AT THE
HEART
OF THE
DEEP

CARRIE L. WELLS

WHR PUBLISHING

WHR Publishing, June 2105

Copyright 2015 Carrie L. Wells

ISBN-13: 978-0692464311

ISBN-10: 069246431X

Published by WHR Publishing
PO Box 100828
Palm Bay, FL 32910
whrpublishing.com
Cover art by Quirky Bird Designs.

For Tony

AT THE

HEART

OF THE

DEEP

ONE: ANYA

THE SMALL SHIP intrigued me. Hundreds of boats cross my path daily, but this one, trailing temperature gauges and current trackers, interested me more than others. Rather than merely floating, this boat had a purpose, a reason to be so close to my island. Of course, the blond man diving into the water definitely had something to do with my interest and maybe the boat's purpose, too. His long, lean body cracked the face of the water, and as he surfaced, his strong arms propelled him forward and away from the boat. Every afternoon he did the same thing, dive, swim, float, swim back. And every afternoon I watched as his fluid movements made almost no break in the ocean's surface while he cut long paths across it.

I had announced to the tribe that we had visitors close, and immediately the chatter began.

Assuring them the boat's and crew's focus was research, or looked to be, I held off further inquisition with a promise to continue tracking their efforts.

I met the boat for five days and each day they came a little closer. Today they sat only twenty miles from Orotava. Close enough that Phoebe and Fiona decided to join me in my afternoon surveillance. The twins heckled me as I led them through the sea. We hung back far enough that their equipment couldn't track our presence.

"It's a long way to go for a man, Anya," Phoebe commented, laughing at me as we swam.

Her sister joined in. "Any distance is too far for a man."

Both knew I'd never had any interest in humans before. I was far more comfortable in the sea than walking on land, even on our own island full of mer. But this one, comfortable in the sea and almost questing to be a part of it, lured me. At the very least, he was lovely to watch and I could fantasize about adding him to my land life.

"Look, neither of you had to come with me. I'm just fine watching this sea god all on my own."

I smirked back at my childhood friends, taunting them with my infatuation.

The three of us surfaced and watched him cut through the waves with capable, powerful movements. He looked at home with the water cradling his body.

"That's some human," Fiona commented, breaking into my daydream.

Phoebe seemed more awed than her appreciative twin. "He's, well, he's beautiful," she added. "Look how smoothly he moves. He's part fish."

"No, he's all human," I concluded. "If he were part fish, I could do more than stare."

"So true," Phoebe agreed. "Unless he was a Trisanthian. Your father would rather unite you with a human."

She had a point. Nishan, my father and the tribal council leader of the Obthaluse, wouldn't stand for his only daughter uniting with a rival mer, but he also wouldn't care much for a human son-in-law.

We continued to watch the boat and the swimmer until he turned and started back. We dove below the waves to be sure he didn't look up and find three gawking mermaids. I pushed the boundaries a lot, but we had never been caught by humans. Maybe today was the day to change that.

From below we saw his tanned legs stir the water and force him forward. His steady pace moved him quickly and we kept at a distance. That gave us a chance to move closer to the drifting boat in order to watch him climb aboard, my favorite part of the last few days. Granted, while my father made plans to attend the united tribal meetings, my research sessions on the island had lengthened, not leaving lots of time for fun.

The man reached the boat and lifted himself onto the diving platform. The sun on his wet hair turned it a golden, tawny yellow, almost the same color as my own.

Fiona let out her breath with a sigh. "Too bad he has legs. Nothing good comes with legs," she explained authoritatively.

Phoebe and I both chuckled a bit. He whipped his head in our direction and we quickly dipped below the surface. He squinted at the ripple we left

AT THE HEART OF THE DEEP

in the water, but he turned away and continued to climb to the deck.

Someone called out to him as he toweled off. "Oh, hey, Luke. Glad you're back. Amir found something we want you to see."

"Luke," I repeated as I exhaled and watched him disappear into the boat's cabin.

"Luke, Luke, Luke," Phoebe chanted in a sing-song voice.

At least I had a name to go with the lovely face.

Fiona joined in. "Not a bad name. It suits him. Luke, the light-giver. Isn't that what it means?," she remarked thoughtfully.

"No idea, but I like it. It fits him," Phoebe added. Then she started singing, "Luke, the light-giver, looks lovely and luscious."

"Phoebe, seriously?" I asked, more than a bit annoyed by my normally sweet friend.

"Wow, Anya, you must really be smitten. You don't get ticked off that easily." She smiled, either at the thought of pushing my buttons or maybe because I was smitten. I'm not sure which, but she would derive pleasure from either scenario.

Pointing at the bow, suddenly, Phoebe added, "Look. The *Sea Star*."

Her sister responded, confused, "What? What about it?"

"It's the name of the boat. The *Sea Star*."

"Okay, and?"

"Well, and nothing really. But it's kind of cute that the boat is the *Sea Star* and Anya has that star mark. And did you see his tattoo? It was a sea star, too."

"Only you would find that cute, Phoebe," Fiona chided. She considered herself the practical twin, while Phoebe held the title of dreamer.

But Fiona was wrong. I noticed the boat's name the first time I followed Luke to it. My father called me *Sea Star*. He used the nickname more often when I was younger, but he resorted to it now and again. He gave me the name when I was born because of the small, star-shaped patch of dark scales on my tail. And now it linked me to Luke. It was such a little thing, but it tied us together in a small way.

"She's dreaming again, Phee."

Phoebe's voice called me back to reality and I watched the boat pick up speed. Fiona swam towards it, taunting us to join her. Not ready to back down, Phoebe and I joined, racing to see who could reach her first.

We came up on the boat quickly, far faster than any of us anticipated. Forgetting about the tracking equipment, we closed the distance, breaching the surface and playing in the waves like dolphin. I hoped that's what we looked like. That way, if anyone glanced bchind the boat, they'd just assume they'd attracted curious dolphins rather than stalking mermaids.

Unexpectedly, Luke reappeared on deck. He looked at the sky, upset, and walked briskly to the stern, reading a tablet. By the time he looked up, Fiona and Phoebe were safe below the churning water. I, however, dove head first over the boat's wake, locking eyes with him in the process. Not the way to go unnoticed.

His deep brown eyes caught mine, holding them, holding me. I didn't look away when he leaned over the railing before climbing down to the dive deck. I knew he saw me. All of me. But in that moment, I wanted him to know. I wanted him to know everything.

TWO: LUKE

"DAMMIT!" I YELLED, bellowing at the sky. I cursed myself and the ocean as yet another storm moved across the horizon. The *Sea Star* wasn't large, and the strong winds and unrelenting rains along Florida's Treasure Coast shook it mercilessly when the summer storms blew in. I hoped the winds would shift and we could avoid the traditional three o'clock rains. The *Sea Star*'s size made it great for our research, but it was also more susceptible to the weather and the ocean than larger vessels.

I ran onto the deck when I noticed dramatic changes in the tracker information. I figured the storms caused the disruption, but the temperature went up noticeably, eleven degrees, and suddenly.

And the current shifted as though something was trailing us.

I had already taken my swim, not wanting the storms to interfere. I crave time with the water. Surfing and diving as a kid, I'm not sure I've spent more than three months of my life at a time without the sand and surf as part of my daily routine. And now, at sea, I swim at least once a day, embracing the waves and feeling unnatural without a hint of salt on my skin. Stir crazy was an understatement after my time gearing up for this trip. While we only left land two weeks earlier, I'd been in a small office full of maps and depth charts for months before the trip. Now my body itched to stretch and move through the water. Spending time in the water was, after all, my motivation to become an oceanographer. That and the girls in the University of Miami's oceanography department looked great in scuba gear.

At the stern, I figured I might find the storm clouds closer than anticipated or maybe the trackers had tangled again. What I found, however, was nothing I foresaw. In fact, what I found wasn't real. It belonged in myth, not in a research log.

But I saw it. I saw her.

"Hey, McAllister," Brandon, my research assistant, echoed in the radio. "Mac? You there, man?"

I had a tendency to forget my radio or just ignore it, so he was definitely right to stalk me when he had news.

"I'm here. What ya got?"

"The radio says to expect the afternoon squall a little early today."

Tearing my eyes from the wake of the boat, I blinked away the image and turned to the clouds.

Looking up at the sky, I radioed back. "Brando, believe 'em. Those clouds look angry."

Ignoring my gut instinct to head back inside, I climbed down to the dive deck, hoping to catch a glimpse of it, of her, again. Instead, the trackers were the only things behind the boat. Maybe I hadn't seen anything at all. We hadn't been at sea long, but strange things happened when men looked into the horizon. Hell, at least I hadn't pissed off Poseidon or landed on an island with a cyclops.

Brandon came down to pull up the trackers.

"Hey, you could help me, ya know," he said, elbowing me as I stood staring at the waves rolling behind us.

"Sorry, man. Distracted. How deep do you think we can see in that wake?"

"Deep? Uh, maybe 15 feet down if the object is a light color, like a shark or a tracker."

Fifteen feet gave me plenty of room to misread what I saw. As a scientist, I knew repeated results were the only way to draw a solid conclusion. One observation, one test, is never enough. Maybe if Brandon had seen her too, had been there to back up my sighting, I would have doubted myself a bit less.

As a scientist charged with researching the shift of ocean depths off the coast of Florida, I studied, theorized, and met with colleagues, all to no avail. The sea was changing, quickly, and that would eventually mean changes for those of us on land, too. All the published research pointed to the many hurricanes and rising ocean levels. Some of it mentioned the fascination tourists have with driving on the beaches and residents' need to build bigger, grander homes on the coast. But I knew there was something more, especially since the beach erosion contributed only a small fraction to the issue. And I managed to convince a few others, the ones with the money, that it was worth a look.

I spent months with my team hypothesizing the lesser known causes. We all determined one thing. The answer lies within the ocean. So we collected the grant, geared up, and set sail.

And now there was her. She didn't fit into this at all. Or maybe she did.

We had been studying the issue for more than a year and this was our second trip out to sea. Heading back underway after what we called the "reset", we were ready to look at different factors than we had before. She fit that category. She was definitely a different factor.

Seeing the clouds turning duskier, Brandon and I headed back up the ladder with the equipment. Amir was on deck now, a head taller than Brandon with dark skin standing out against the white of the boat.

"Just in time, guys. You know dark clouds come in fast," Amir commented.

Then I noticed the winds picking up. Heading to the cabin, we stashed the equipment. The deck was not the place to be when you were off the coast of Lightning Alley and the skies turned black.

Amir reached into an overhead compartment, stowing equipment he had been tinkering with. The Detroit-native's long arms saved the team on a few occasions when equipment had gotten beyond our reach. Brandon's stocky build, on the other hand, shrouded the strength of someone twice his size, earning him the nickname "Ant" when we wanted to rile him.

The boat's weather alarm blared suddenly, "Whooooop, whooooop, whooooop."

Lucy slipped past us, grabbing her laptop and gliding to a table. The graduate assistant was young and focused. I liked her quick wit and her fast, mouse-like behaviors as she constantly moved around the boat. We filed in behind her.

While run down and cluttered, the *Sea Star's* interior was comfortable. From inside, we watched fat droplets hit the windows, splattering like paint. At this point, water and sky mirrored each other, both dark and menacing at that point, marching along the horizon. With nothing left to do, I picked up the old deck of cards. In that moment, I had to face that I would never let her slip from my mind with the same ease she used as she slid from my view.

THREE: ANYA

I SPOTTED THE boat as it moved overhead the next day. As I swam out towards it, I noticed its glistening hull, its props churning a silvery froth. I knew they were closer to the island. I knew my father and the counsel wouldn't welcome them. I knew the entire tribe may be in danger. I knew Luke had seen me. But I kept swimming.

Complacency had gotten the best of me after a long few months not leaving the boundaries of the island of Orotava. Our secluded island was quiet. Mer life was peaceful. There is never anything to avoid there. Unmapped islands don't attract much attention. I'd spent most of my time cooped up in my research lab on the island trying to explain the changes in our native waters. Once in a while I'd visit the trench, looking for a reason or rhyme behind the sudden changes, but today was different.

Today, I decided to run down a boat, a boat with an appealing, swimming sailor. A sailor I was sure hadn't understood what he saw. I would become another mirage in the waves. One of those things he could easily write off as a trick of light on the water.

The tribal scouts reported the boat when it was more than 25 leagues away. Nishan, knowing about the boat, forbade me from going anywhere near it.

"Anya," he said in his authoritative voice, "let me remind you, lest you have forgotten, that your research must lead you to the deep and not to the surface — or to anything that may come from it."

However, I needed to know if the boat or the equipment, the devices they'd been trailing through the water, related to my own research and what we found beyond the reef.

"If you feel the need to swim constantly, at least remain deep enough to avoid attention. That boat is getting far too close to our island. Do not investigate. I'll receive a report tonight at the festival, Anya, and I do not expect to hear your name associated with it. Do not ignore me," he said.

Warm he isn't. But I always know where I stand with my father.

I shocked him with my unusually quiet response. "Yes, father. I'll see you tonight."

THE FESTIVAL OF the Fourteen Seas began hours after I returned from my research. As I swam through the garland-strewn reef, approaching the bay, my eyes feasted on the color and gaiety of the day. Seaweed draped the red and orange corals of my lovely Atlantic home.

The sunken pirate schooner, the *Scarlet Witch*, turned green by algae, sat dressed in ribbons of pink and white scallop shells shining in the dispersed sunlight. Barnacles laced through and across the planks. Pearls shown in strands draped from the mast. The effect was ethereal and everything seemed to glow.

The tides would turn for 31 days throughout the festival, and we would pay tribute to each of the seas. Then, at the festival's final ceremony, we would learn of the news of each tribal nation.

The Obthaluse, my tribe and Orotava's founders, had plans to reveal new developments in our research, my research. Although we had no definite findings, we did have preliminary information that could change our world drastically. Nishan had finally been convinced that we needed to share that information with the Coalition of

Tribes. To me, our declaration was nerve-wracking; however, it was the news the other tribes would release that panicked others.

Tribes revealed everything from new land acquisitions to changes in counsel leadership. In the bad years, wars started. In the good years, alliances were made and treaties signed. This event dictated relationships between tribes and the goings on for the next year.

While we celebrated the festival in Orotava each year, the greater Coalition would meet in the Aegean Sea. This year the Garceaenians would play host to the festival and counsel leaders, including my father, prepared for their travels.

The counsel gathered to discuss the ebbing, as we called the information reveal, for months prior to the festival. Then, as the reveling began, the Coalition called upon the Nereids to further direct their decisions. The daughters of Nereus and Doris were ready to prove their prowess this ebbing cycle. Having swum the seas hundreds of years before merfolk existed, the sea nymphs controlled quite a bit of the ocean. Luckily, we catered well to the ocean daughters, and we allowed for the traditions of the Nereids, including the festival.

The Nereids oversaw the ebbing, adjudicating the ceremony for the Coalition and mediations throughout the year. Granted, fights erupted between the nymphs often, as with any sisters, and that could make for an interesting ebbing. While the festivities were underway, the celebration would be the only thing anyone focused on in the mer community. Every choice or plan in our tribes, in our lives, would depend on the ebbing. Unfortunately, that meant our lives and worlds also depended on the political and personal alliances of the Nereids.

Tonight my father would hold the festival's opening ceremonies, making his speech to the tribe before heading to the ebbing. And as always, the festival began in the sea.

As the tribe gathered at our reef, Nishan appeared, ready to address our colony and scanning the crowd. Regal with his long white beard, he held court on the deck of the sunken ship. Searching, his eyes found their target — me.

"Alavay," he began, using our traditional welcome. "Mer of the Obthaluse tribe, tonight marks our 700th Festival of the Fourteen Seas, a chance to pay tribute to our past, our tribal history. Tonight marks our continuation, as well as a chance to go beyond our past. As we rejoice and come together, let us not forget those who have changed our current and shifted the tides of our tribe."

At that point the tribe cheered. I joined them. The festival, always a favorite of mine, was kicking off nicely.

Nishan continued, "Tonight we feast, we revel, we remember. We thank the seas. We celebrate our unity. We pray peace continues between the tribes. And we welcome. We welcome our futures, embracing the unforeseen opportunities that lie before us.

"In three days' time, the Coalition will convene. We will sit together with the Nereids asking them to bless the declarations we make. As the tides turn throughout the lunar cycle, all tribes will ebb. But tonight, tonight the Obthaluse rejoice."

He pulled a strand of strung shells and a rainbow of small seahorses swam about, swirling upward in waves of color and motion.

After shaking hands and accepting general congratulations, Nishan sought me in the crowd. His robust torso, complete with broad shoulders, controlled a powerful ebony tail. Stippled with scales, it caught the sun with a metallic shimmering effect. An imposing force and monumental presence, others offered him respect by bearing alone, and thus he expected it. I learned to respect him as a leader, but I loved him as my father.

I nodded goodbye to Phoebe and Fiona. We had spent every opening ceremony together since our birth, and I planned to enjoy the festival with them later. Drudgingly, I swam in my father's direction. He noticed and excused himself from the crowd.

"Anya." He addressed me stoically. No one overhearing us would think he was speaking to his daughter as his formal tone erased any familiarity.

"Alavay, Father."

"It seems this boat, these people, are measuring the currents, their speeds and distances. They may be taking temperatures, as well. While it appears there was nothing malicious, nothing out of the ordinary in their equipment or actions. You are to remain hidden. If this means a pause in your research, so be it."

"Father, I can't do that. This research is too important. We still don't know why this is happening, where the energy is coming from, and whether any of it is detrimental to Orotava, to the tribe."

"This is not a debate. They are close, far too close. This is not something I can tolerate right now. And I'm not asking you to avoid them. I demand that you do."

"But they aren't headed towards Orotava. They have no business here," I tried to explain, already defending a man I didn't know.

"Can you be sure of that?" he asked, visibly unnerved.

I took a moment to answer. "Well, no, but they're researchers, not cartographers. Not a mining company. They aren't tracking animals that would bring them to the island. I think they're okay. Really."

"I'm not so sure, and I'm wondering how you know so much about this boat." He shook his head in frustration. "But for now," he replied far more gently than I expected, "you and your friends enjoy the festival." He bent and brushed a kiss on my forehead before rejoining the group of lingering mer.

Confused by the exchange, I turned to see if Phoebe and Fiona were anywhere close. Not seeing them, I swam away from the *Vengeful Dane*. I needed some time to process the conversation and what I'd do next.

F O U R :   L U K E

I VIVIDLY RECALLED the tail and eyes as I woke the next few mornings and many times throughout the day. I dreamt of her at least three times that night. Her beautiful tail gleamed in the sun and it matched her bright eyes. The eyes. The eyes shared nothing with any aquatic creature I knew. The color belonged in a jeweler's case. The shape was human, or at least mammalian. Blue eyes. No, green eyes. Neither was right. Eyes the color of my mother's birthstone, aquamarine maybe. I'd figure that out when I decided to face reality. Eventually, I'd have to admit I had seen a mermaid.

I knew I wasn't insane and had seen something in those waves. It did everything but wave at me. And if it, she, had waved, I could at least consider it a delusion. But people see things in the ocean. The water creates mysteries or there would be no stories of the Kraken or Atlantis. So how did one awkward vision leave me dreaming and questioning? The dream was the same and the most realistic dream of my life. A blur of sea foam and ginger hair, all yellow-gold and honey hued.

"I have the latest reads. I know you hav-," Brandon started, entering the monitor room. He stopped, seeing the flustered look on my face.

Startling me out of my memory, Brandon pulled me back to the world and what was left of my sanity. Confused, I stared, part scowl, part "Huh?"

"Great. Anything?" I asked, pulling myself together.

"Nothing big. A few bumps here and there," Brandon went on, reading the data. "Well, that's weird. Look."

He handed me the readout. The graph contained one series of large spikes far higher than the others.

"Whatever it was got close to the boat," I explained. "Not too large though."

"Like turtle not large or small whale not large?"

"Probably dolphin-sized," I said, putting Brandon at ease. Brandon had a fear of being capsized. Anything bigger than a dolphin rolling around the boat, toying with it, would certainly leave him with nightmares. Granted, I'd rather he think a megalodon was eying us for dinner than admit to being followed by a mermaid.

"Thank Posiedon for that," Brandon joked. "Got anything else for me, Mac?"

"Nothing, man. Nothing. Time to take a break."

"You coming up?" he asked. We sometimes grabbed a few beers on deck on clear nights. Nothing but the sea, the stars, and the suds.

"I'll be up. Give me a few."

As Brandon left, I considered the readings again. Something about six feet long had interfered with the equipment's readings. I based my career on the idea that data couldn't lie. It didn't make judgments. It couldn't manipulate.

So.

She must exist. She must have come back and disrupted the readings again.

But, that was impossible.

I found it difficult to think about her as "her". But she clearly was. The golden hair, pale breasts, and curve of her back all led to that conclusion. But since she wasn't real, whatever I thought she was didn't matter.

I sat at the computer, watching the monitors, the radar. I stared at the cursor as I debated a simple Internet search. Knowing that the searches on board weren't saved — we had limited memory and didn't care if what the crew searched in their down time — I held my breath and typed M-E-R-M-A-I-D-S. Google spit out more than 100 million results. Videos and pictures, web sites and items for sale. Where to go from there?

I scrolled through the pictures of anime-style mermaids, doe-eyed females with long hair, large breasts, and green scaled tails instead of legs. I saw lifelike mermaids drawn to resemble tailed women without the cartoon quality enhancements. I looked at the real, live mermaids who inhabited swimming and diving shows throughout Florida. None of them looked like her.

I shut my eyes, envisioning her beautiful hair. The golden hair the colors of ginger. Pale and sunny yellows blended with beige and darker browns. It created a shimmering web I pictured floating around her. Her shoulders were the same pallor as mine when I spent too much time in an office with a shirt on. And her face. So delicate that I could see the pink blush on her cheeks when she spotted me.

I had seen far more of her than I initially thought. As she twisted to dive, after we locked eyes, I glimpsed red gill openings below her ribcage. The water fluttered past them and her breasts rose and fell. I noticed the scales scattered on her arms and torso, not like the clearly half-fish-half-women online. The transition from woman to fish with her was clear, but not abrupt. Her hips, while part of her tail, were clearly woman-like in form and emphasized by the shadowing of scales. A leg outline could be seen beneath the tale as if the scales had grown over a human form and joined legs together. And there was a small, blue-black star on her tail. The shape was made up of dark scales that almost glittered in the sun.

While I quickly acknowledged my memories of her, I still eagerly dismissed her existence.

When I joined the crew, our conversation focused on the day's sudden data changes. Seeing temperature shifts was normal, but they had been far more gradual than those recorded in the last two days. The current shifts showed a large disruption, but as Brandon and I figured, it was most likely an animal.

And as I figured, a mermaid.

"I think we should focus on the temperature spike," Kate, another researcher on the team, offered.

Amir nodded in agreement, grabbing a soda from the mini fridge. I motioned for one too and caught the can he tossed.

Kate continued, "How the hell did we go up more than eleven degrees in two minutes?"

We all sat, thinking, until Lucy bounded into the room. It seemed the entire crew needed a cold caffeine fix at the same time. She was grabbing for the mini fridge door and listening as the conversation continued.

"We've seen increases before. But this was drastic," I answered as I reached out with my foot and shut the fridge for Lucy.

"I figured you'd have brought up the data variances before now," she commented with a slight smile. "You guys must have been busy."

Amir flipped her pony tail playfully, a big brother gesture. "We have. It's that damn chore wheel you make us use. I was doing dishes."

"Not my fault you can't multitask, O' Tall One," she stated while bowing regally to Amir.

Brandon interrupted their fun, interjecting, "The tracker's placement may have upset the data a bit, but that shouldn't be any different than any other day. What were you thinking, Kate?"

"Well, there are pockets of temperature shifts. We know that. We've seen that data. But those recordings look different." She pulled out a record of our findings. "If you look at this, the previous shift, the one four days ago, was gradual, over seven minutes, and it hit a full eight degrees higher. But that was at a 20 foot depth, not 75."

I poured over the paper with Amir and Lucy moving in to see it well. Studying the chart did nothing for me, though. I knew what changed the temperature. I saw the cause. But there was no way I was admitting to it right now.

"What about the current shift? What do we think caused that?" Brandon said.

"Weren't we close to that manatee breeding area?" Lucy asked frowning, her brows getting closer together. "I know it is miles away, but it could have been a manatee, or more than one."

Kate considered the question before answering, "No, we weren't close enough for that. And there isn't any land mapped, so they weren't coming from a marina somewhere else. This is just too deep for most of them since it isn't migration season."

"Well, dolphins have followed us before," Amir affirmed. "I'm sure they could screw with the current pattern like that. Maybe with the temperature if there were enough of them."

"Dolphins don't screw with things," Lucy interjected fiercely. "They may alter the data, but they don't screw with it."

Her dolphin obsession didn't make her the most unbiased researcher at times, but since we didn't research dolphins, it was more of a charming idiosyncrasy than a threat to our findings.

I thought for a few minutes and then offered a theory. While I knew it was wrong, I figured at least it would delay their frustration a bit. "What if there was an issue with the tracker? Maybe it is a false recording."

"Two of them at the same time?" Kate questioned.

Amir shook his head. "Nah. That can't be it. Too much of a fluke."

"We did have that surge last night," Brandon threw in.

The power surge was small, but it had taken us all by surprise, but I hadn't given it much consideration after seeing her. I did need to look into it, though.

As far as I was concerned, a few questions still existed, but I was willing to give up a day of research to testing the equipment in order avoid saying what I knew.

"So now what?" Lucy asked the group.

"Time to test," Kate said, nodding at the research. "Again."

FIVE: ANYA

AFTER THE CEREMONY, we reveled in the sea for two more days, as was our custom. On the fourth day, we swam below to a dark opening in the caves. The water broke around the sharp edges, camouflaging an entrance to those who didn't already know of its existence.

The inside of the cave had a high ceiling only half filled with churning sea water. The water pressure lessened as we swam through the cave into a larger one with less water. The series of caves allowed our bodies to adjust to life on land. The caves allowed our lungs to expand and become useful, our gills to close, and our legs to develop. The final cave included only a tidal pool and exited on a tree-lined beach. The transitioning beach, ensconced by trees, gave us a chance to practice our land legs before we got into town.

Orotava is a small island, only about 3,000 square miles. Smaller even than Puerto Rico. The reef on the southern side offers shelter from approaching ships, and rocks climb up the Eastern side, silvery black and slick. We are protected in a number of ways from outsiders and generally at ease.

As I walked across the beach, hot sand stroking my new toes and sun caressing my naked skin, I wasn't at ease, however. I was focused on my research, worrying about the trench and what might have changed in my days celebrating. I stumbled a bit and fell into a tall merman I hadn't seen in months. Gregorio, a friend of mine for many years, had been away on ambassador missions, working with the Garceaenians. He caught me quickly, traipsing along without issue. He walked beside me using lengthy strides. I watched the small scales on his upper body, a bright, deep blue, minimize as we crossed the beach. By the time we reached the vegetation line, neither of us had scales showing anywhere and my footing was solid.

Hidden amid the trees at the beach line were small changing cabanas, offering transitional clothing to mer heading out of the sea. Naked, we slipped into the cabanas; groups of us emerged in bright, summery clothing, ready to once again participate in life on land.

Gregorio met up with me as I exited my cabana. We walked down the cobblestone path catching up on his travels.

"Anya, you would love the Norwegian and Aegean Seas," he said. "The parties are amazing. Gorgeous mermaids and plenty of lavish dinners where the vodka flowed through ice.. You'd fit in beautifully. And the hours I spent in Istanbul, sitting around the raki table. If I could only remember the things I did on those nights."

He laughed at his own joke, and while arrogant, his travels still intrigued me. They sounded glorious, something straight out of a fantasy. He even offered to bring me with him at some point. And that surprised me almost as much as my consideration of the idea.

Traveling those distances was something I had often considered, but Gregorio was never a part of my future plans. Friends for years, I never saw him that way before. But the sea was changing, and maybe that meant I should change a little too. Besides, thinking of the hunky merman could only help me avoid thoughts of Luke.

As we walked, I noticed how salt coated every surface. The sun baked it into the surrounding facades bleaching them. The buildings appeared water colored compared to the vivid shocks of colored fabric we wore. The breeze lifted gulls high above us and blew through the palmetto fronds, lifting the smell of tropical flowers — hibiscus, gardenia, and jasmine especially. He reached out into the green leaves, snapped off a dramatic fuchsia hibiscus blossom, and tucked it behind my left ear.

"Beautiful," he remarked. "The perfect touch. You are captivating. I'm glad to have come across you today, Anya."

"Thank you," I replied, not knowing what else to say.

"We should catch up. I have plenty to share with you about my visit to the Indian Ocean. I think you'd be interested. I know I'd be willing to do it over dinner if that works for you."

Was he angling for a date? I didn't have time to consider a life-long acquaintance as a love interest at this point. I had research to do.

"Oh that does sound great, but I think I'll head to the lab now. No need to walk with me. I know you're a busy mer," I assured him. Maybe I was too abrupt.

He shook off a sudden look of confusion, asking, "Why is that? There are still weeks left in the festival. No one will be at the lab."

"I just need to look in on things. I'm sure it's all fine, but I'd feel more comfortable checking in."

Gregorio nodded as if he understood.

"Beautiful and brilliant," he said smoothly, leaning forward, surprising me with a soft and purposeful kiss.

With my cheeks suddenly flush, I looked away. Taken aback by the kiss, something felt odd. It didn't seem the time nor place for a first kiss.

Sensing my embarrassment, he shifted the topic. "Tomorrow is another day, Anya. Why don't you wait and I'll accompany you to the lab after the party tonight. Rowan has opened the tavern, my brother's band is playing, and everyone will be looking for you there."

He smiled as we turned down a smaller lane, my lane. At the end of the short avenue stood my quaint cottage. Covered in aged siding, the grayed exterior was a splendid backdrop to a yard of flowering shrubs. Small, bright blooms dotted dark green bushes that seemed to hover above the sandy ground. Yellows, pinks, oranges, and whites seeped from the foliage and clouded the air. Flowers were my favorite part of being on land, so I made sure to surround my home with them.

"That's yours, right?" He pointed at the bungalow with its flower garden and peaked roof. The white trimmed porch held a red door that beckoned to me.

"Yep, that's me." I hadn't expected to be so happy to be on land, but in that moment, I couldn't see how any other dwelling would be more agreeable than the one standing in front of me.

As we approached my small home, and Gregorio mentioned, "The festivities will kick off around 7 tonight. The tavern will be full, I'm sure, and I'd love to accompany you. There is nothing I'd like more than to have the whole tribe see me in such wonderful company."

Live music and plenty of dancing would set the stage for a wonderful festival on land the same way the opening ceremony did in the sea. I knew the details of the night as well as he did, but I assumed he was just used to knowing things and reporting them. While I tried not to take his informative tone personally, it irked me a little to be treated like a guest on my own island.

"I'll be there. In fact, I'm meeting Phoebe and Fiona, but I'll be sure to look for you," I said trying to avoid the commitment of a date at this point.

I opened the door and he escorted me in but demurely remained in my foyer. Claiming exhaustion, I promised to see him later that night.

"Oh, Anya, I don't mind if you rest. Maybe we could rest together," he suggested.

I couldn't hide my surprise at his forwardness, so I didn't try. "Gregorio, stop it," I said flirtily. I wasn't ready to close the door on him as an option, just on him in my house right then.

As he left, I excitedly settled back into my home.

I had never lived alone before I took the cottage. But with the hours I spent at the lab and in the sea, it made sense to live alone and as close as possible to both. The idea of three enclosed rooms just for me made my head spin initially. But I had furnished it nicely, warmly, and it felt as much like home as my father's house had as I grew up. I walked in, running my hand along the mahogany table the color of Fiona's hair, the wide, white chair rail, the wallpaper covered in the tiniest pink rose buds. I was in love with the cottage and wondered why I had been so hell bent on spending time at sea lately when I had this here.

But there wasn't much time to enjoy my home. As I sat on my bed, I realized Gregorio had steered me home instead of to my lab. With the new information floating in my mind, I decided to give my legs a break and lie down a bit before going to the lab.

SIX: LUKE

I FELT BADLY watching the crew work so hard testing the equipment when I knew there was nothing wrong with it. Considering the other option, confessing why I knew the equipment wasn't at fault, I let them waste a few days. We didn't have much to do otherwise, so we sat, hovering in one spot as not to miss any collectible data.

Kate pouted her way through another testing cycle.

"All five tests have shown this tracker's working. I don't understand. No variance at all," she explained.

Amir lugged in another tracker. "I'd call it a day, Kate. You're going to make yourself crazy. Besides, the others were all working, too. So maybe it wasn't the tracker."

"George will be so disappointed to hear this is all we've done this week."

"The little man will understand. Or just tell the kid something exciting. Tell him how Lucy kicked Brando's ass when he drank her Pepsi," I said laughing.

She wasn't impressed by my idea. "Absolutely inappropriate. Hilarious, but inappropriate. You do remember he's only six, right?"

Maybe it had been inappropriate, but she was right. It had been hilarious. Lucy launched herself out of her chair when Brandon grabbed the last cold Pepsi. I still don't know how she did it, but she had him in a head lock at one point, her feet not even touching the floor anymore. All this happened as she vehemently pointed out her name in black marker on the side of the can.

"Do you see that," she bellowed. "Look! L-U-C-Y. Yep, that's Lucy, ya fool."

Brandon, knowing he'd been beaten, begged for mercy, crying uncle like kids did in grade school, and handed her the open can. After conceding, he leaned over and opened a 24-pack of warm soda and refilled the fridge, adding insult to Lucy's injury.

"Let's take the trackers out back. We'll see if we can replicate the issue. Maybe that will make Kate feel better," I threw out as Norton, our captain, walked in.

"You guys gotta get up on deck and see something," he said quietly. Norton normally walked and talked with far more gusto than he displayed at the moment.

Obviously shaken, he sat down, not making eye contact with any of us, and clearly not planning to head on deck.

We filed out solemnly, equally worried and anxious to see what had thrown our salty dog captain off balance. Emerging on deck, we noticed small balls of light fluttering around the *Sea Star*.

"Lighting bugs?" Brandon asked.

"If you mean fire flies, no," Lucy concluded. "They can't fly this far out to sea."

Kate took a minute for offering a sensible, thought-out hypothesis. "Maybe they're airborne, glowing plankton. They could be hovering in the water vapor."

We all looked at her in amazement as her mind conjured up a new species or one whose lifestyle adapted to humid air faster than the rest of us formed thoughts.

Standing there silent, we gawked. As we stared, the flecks of light seemed to attract to one another, forming golf ball-sized groups instead of what we assumed were single entities. Hovering over the boat, bouncing off the waves, the balls tripped along.

Amir reached out to touch one. He was rewarded by a sharp reprimand from Kate and an equally sharp, be it small, electric shock. Looking at his finger, he saw no tissue damage, but it tingled where he had contacted the energy ball.

Norton ventured onto the deck at that point and asked one question, "What do your studies say about that, Luke?"

SEVEN: ANYA

I WOKE WITH a start hours later. The sky had grown dark, but it was not yet night. Gray clouds moved quickly above my cottage and the wind picked up with low bellows.

I noticed the time and checked the mirror quickly. I looked the same on land as I did in the sea. My hair shown with the same shades of sun and sand even though it was dry. My eyes glowed a bright aquamarine that normally matched my fins. My skin remained pale, a pearly contrast to the rich blue shade I wore.

Running, something I hadn't done recently, out of the cottage, the ambrosia my flowers released at my door embraced me. I stopped long enough to pluck a jasmine bud and tuck into my hair. I liked the idea of Gregorio seeing it in the same spot where he put the hibiscus earlier, which felt odd. I hadn't planned to enjoy his company in that way, and I truly didn't have time or energy to spare right now. Yet, I was tucking flowers with the hope that he would notice.

I had spent far too much daydreaming of Luke. He wasn't an option, and I knew my father, the tribe actually, had plenty to say of humans. Why waste time dreaming when a perfectly gorgeous mer was waiting for me?

Nearing the Sword and Dagger Tavern, having abandoned the idea of spending time in the lab, I heard music, singing, and laughing. Feeling excited and bold, I pranced into the party, into the group of friends and relatives. I spotted Uncle Jinsen. Thrilled to see him, I ran to him, my arms out for a hug. My mother's brother, Uncle Jinsen was a favored friend from my childhood. He had played with me and entertained my childish antics. Having no children, he and my aunt had always treated me as their own.

"Anya, my dear niece, hug me again," he clamored. I wrapped my arms around him yet again. "That's what was missing, everyone. Anya. Anya was missing. But, she's here now. And a good time we will have."

He handed me a glass of sweet juices mixed with a strong coconut flavor. Rum punch. It smelled heavenly and cut through the taste of salt in the humid air. I finished the drink only to have Gregorio there and handing me another.

"I'm happy you made it, Anya," he confided.

"Well, I'm happy to find you," I admitted, realizing it was true. I was happy that Gregorio wanted me at the party.

We sat together, his long legs reaching out in front of him while I curled mine up under me. We chatted about the day and he apprised me of his latest travels. He had been circling the seas as assistant to the ambassador, my uncle. They'd been gone for months, sharing news and research with other tribes, helping the host tribe prepare for the festival, and participating in goodwill endeavors.

"Anya, you would love traveling. I know you've done some with your father, but traveling as an ambassador's assistant brings you to such amazing places. I've seen the dirty rivers of New York and the blue waters of Fiji. You can't begin to believe the places I've been," he continued.

Excited to hear about his adventures at first, his continued droning on and on coupled with the alcohol left me sleepy. The music pounded, but my eyes drooped a bit more with every glass Gregorio had ready for me.

He introduced me to a few more glasses of rum punch before the evening wound down. My head swam with warmth and the perfume of the island and the look in his eyes. His face softened when he looked at me.

But it was the stars that amazed me. Mer often went to the surface while in the sea, seeing both the moon and sun. We drifted and played in the waves with the seals, whales, and gulls. But the sky while on land was distinct. Maybe it was due to the sounds of the land mixing with the sea. Or perhaps the feel of air and legs and sand changed my view of the world.

The evening and the party wound down and I found myself disappointed. As I said my goodbyes, hugging Uncle Jinsen, Gregorio came up behind me.

"I'd like to walk you home," he started. "There are some things we need to discuss"

He politely pointed me in the direction of my home when my first instinct was to turn the wrong way exiting the party.

Laughing, he smirked, "An example of those legendary research skills?"

"Uh, well, I've never researched after rum punch," I reasoned, laughing a bit myself.

We walked, chatting carelessly, until we were far enough from the party that the only sound was the sea crashing against the beach. At that point, Gregorio stopped walking.

He sat me down on a bench and asked me to explain my research.

"I need to know what you know, Anya," he said.

"My research is important. The trench, the sudden and deep break in the ocean's floor holds keys to our future as mer and as Obthalusians.

"If the trench continues to broaden, the ground around Orotava could become unstable. The tides and currents could become stronger, ultimately pulling our lovely island apart."

He didn't appear impressed with my work. Instead, he sat back, fiddling with the stem of a flower he'd picked as we walked.

He stifled a yawn and asked, "And how likely is all of that?"

"I'm not sure yet. But I won't be sure unless I continue my research," I tried to explain. "If I just stop now and the trench continues, we could easily lose everything."

"That won't be the case," he said. "I'm sure you're making far too much of it all."

The discussion tore me from the quiet excitement I felt throughout the day. It left even more questions unanswered. Why would he ask me about my research if he planned to discount it so quickly? What was he trying to do, keep me from the lab? Did Luke fit into this? Did any of this put him in danger? But I didn't ask any of those questions.

Instead, I leaned forward, my head light from the rum, and looked into Gregorio's eyes. I figured now was the time to take a risk. If nothing in my life was going to make sense, my love life might as well be confusing too.

With that in mind, I tilted my head a bit, leaned in, and kissed him.

EIGHT: LUKE

As SUDDENLY AS the balls of energy appeared, they disappeared. In their wake came a storm. It came upon the *Sea Star* quickly and without sympathy. We pulled in all of our equipment, locked down what we could, and hunkered down in the cabin. The computers showed a haze of green on the radars. The rain planned to continue its relentless bombarding of the ship.

"Another round?" I asked unconvincingly, lifting the cards. However, restless after the earlier light show and full of questions, Texas Hold 'Em held little draw at this point.

"Luke, you can't be serious." Brandon retorted with a chuckle.

I flipped the deck at him mid-shuffle, hitting Lucy's arm with more than half of the cards. We turned from the cards to coffee, trying to laugh and chat easily without much to say. No one wanted to talk about the light, so we all processed the incident internally.

Kate, knowing we needed some kind of distraction, turned a bag of cereal into decadent marshmallow treats, and Amir and Brandon had no trouble eating most of them as the rain continued.

The ship lurched and leaned as the waves rose and weather surged. Eventually we turned to bed and I took my shift at the wheel.

"Hey, Norton," I called.

Norton turned to acknowledge me. "Your turn already, big man?" he asked.

"Yes, siree, Cap'n. Time for you to get some shut eye. But grab whatever is left in the galley. Kate made your favorites, and Amir may have left one."

"Well then, what a fine night. Leaving the bridge after a good song is good luck, ya know," Norton joked. Full of seaworthy wisdom, he had a superstitious rule for everything. I was just happy to see he had recovered a bit from our earlier adventure. If anything, he was faking it well.

He handed me the log book after signing himself out. Together we reviewed the course and the weather scan again together.

"Looks like you're in for a long night, Lucas." Norton was the only one other than my grandmother that got away with calling me by my full name. "Thanks for taking over. A man facing this much Mother Nature needs to be wide awake, and that is something I am not."

"I drew the short straw, man. Can't say this is my favorite weather to deal with. I'd rather have an expert at the wheel, but as you're entitled to a break," I said punching at the man's arm, "I'll have to do."

Smiling his sideways smile, Norton punched my arm in return, tapped the *Sea Star* insignia over the door, and almost skipped off the bridge.

I turned to the task at hand, steering the *Sea Star* and keeping course in the midst of a storm. The sky and sea reached into each other, one stretching its fingers down, the other lurching upward, and the rain bridging the two. The vessel and all she contained rocked with the rhythm of the sea, and I held steady. It grew darker as the sun finally fell below the horizon and the clouds covered the stars and moon.

"Thank God for GPS." Sailors once navigated by astrological charts. Celestial bodies were a great back up, but only when you could see them.

Making sure to double check the radar, I contemplated how to avoid the storm. However, the green ribbons on the radar offered no choice other than to stay on course and hope that the surges remained small and clustered.

My good fortune quickly changed.

The boat's antenna shone brightly with a blue flame. St. Elmo's fire. I'd seen it plenty, the plasma lighting the heavens. But what followed was new.

"Holy crap," I yelled. A blue glow lit the sky as it floated about. It seemed to come from the sea, not the sky above, not the antenna. It grew from the size of a golf ball to that of a basketball, buoying through the air and suddenly splitting into half a dozen glowing orbs. They spread out across the blue-black blanket blinding me as they moved.

"Luke, you okay?" Norton echoed over the intercom after hearing my surprise.

"I'm fi-" I began, but all the captain heard was the loud thud as I dropped to the floor.

Norton grabbed Brandon and rushed to the bridge. Throwing open the door, Brandon stepped over my unconscious body and bent to check my pulse. Norton, mesmerized by the drifting lights, even bigger than those we saw earlier, leaned on the intercom and called the rest of the crew to the bridge without changing his gaze.

Kate reached the bridge and gasped. "What the hell is that? What is it?" she pleaded, the timbre of her voice as haunting as the orbs.

"I've no damn idea," was all Norton could spit out before the orbs collided and the entire crew crashed to the boat's deck.

THE LIGHT CUT through the haze in my head as I opened my eyes. Pain. The throbbing in my head took over every thought. I tried to remember why I was face down on the floor of the bridge, but nothing came to me. Sitting up, I noticed Brandon. Kate and Norton were on the other side of the bridge.

"What the hell happened?" I asked aloud.

"I'm not sure, but jeez, my head." I heard Lucy's voice, faint, but close.

"Luce, where are you?" I called out, my own voice echoing in my ears loudly.

"I'm by the door. I think I'm alright. But my head," she winced. "Jeez, it hurts."

"Hold on. I'm trying to get up."

"Trying?" she questioned. "Are you hurt?"

"No, I don't think so. My head is swimming. Is your head doing that? God, I'm gonna hurl. Man, what happened?"

"Luke?" Kate's murmur was low and trembling.

"Kate, don't move. I'm coming."

I shakily got my feet beneath me and stood up. Patting myself down, I didn't notice any obvious injuries other than the headache.

As I stepped across the bridge, over Norton's prostrated but breathing body, I saw Lucy and Kate moving slowly. Each appeared unharmed as I looked them over. At that point, Amir, Brandon, and Norton began stirring.

"Worst hangover ever. I didn't even drink," Brandon mumbled, testing his voice.

"I've never seen anything like that," Norton explained. "In all my time on the water, nothing even close."

"St. Elmo's gone wrong?" Brandon asked the captain.

"Nah, not possible. St. Elmo's comes from the sky, not the sea. This burst right out of the ocean."

"It did?" Lucy questioned. "Are you kidding?"

"One minute there was lightning. That alone was bizarre. But the next it looked like something had balled it all up and threw it back to the sky. Something down there was playing baseball with the stuff," I said.

"I just remember seeing a bunch of little lights moving. And then that noise. Like a train hit a building. Metal on metal," Amir added.

"Light doesn't make noise. Not at this level," I mentioned, although each of them knew that fact already.

After ensuring no one had lasting damage, we turned our concern to the research vessel. The *Sea Star* appeared unharmed physically. Her systems were a different issue. We noticed the engines wouldn't turn over and the electrical systems were fried..

"Damn nav system is shot too, Luke," he confirmed.

"Well, it's not like electricity shooting from the ocean wasn't going to screw with something," Kate lectured. "At least we're all fine."

"You're right. But how long have we been drifting?" Lucy asked with hesitation.

Amir looked to the distance. "Long enough to find land," he said pointing into the darkness.

NINE: ANYA

GREGORIO PULLED BACK from the kiss. He was still holding my hands. "Anya, I never imagined this would happen tonight," he said, catching his breath.

"Well, this wasn't on my agenda, really." I leaned in hoping to feel his lush lips on mine a bit more. But as he moved forward to meet me, my attention turned to the sky beyond the bounds of the reef.

From our seat on the island, Gregorio and I could see orbs flaring upward from the sea and dancing in the darkness. They were large and nothing I'd seen before. I knew the trench contained an odd light source, and I did my best to document it. But tonight light flew from the sea. It lit the bay enough for us to see a small boat.

Gregorio pointed at the craft and asked, "Where did that come from? Has anyone reported it?"

"The light?"

"Yes, the light. Where is it coming from?"

"We know it's coming from the ocean's floor. But that's about it," I explained. I wasn't willing to try for the details after the party and the punch.

A metallic noise broke our conversation as specks of light collided sending a vibration through the night. "Did that come from the trench? Is that what you're saying?

"Honestly, Gregorio, I'm not sure what I'm saying at all at this point. I think I may have had a bit too much to drink tonight."

"Think, Anya. Is that something the ocean is generating, or is it something we can contain? Why did it crash like that?"

Suddenly my research seemed important to him. He wasn't yawning now.

I tried to focus on his questions, but the heat of the night and the noise from the impact hit me suddenly.

"I'm not sure what that was. I've never seen it act like that before. I'm tired and I'm drunk and it didn't seem to do any damage. I can't explain anything else."

"Let's just get you inside then. No need to discuss this nonsense any further tonight."

He walked me to my door, opening it for me and ushering me inside. I went straight to the kitchen for a glass of water, suddenly feeling a bit woozy and overwhelmed. I wondered if it was the kiss, the collision of light I witnessed, or the rum.

"Can I get you anything?" I called to Gregorio.

I turned and ran directly into his chest.

Peering down as I wavered against him, he chuckled. I'm sure I looked foolish, but his laughter made me uncomfortable. There was something condescending about his attitude that I had brushed off before but which truly bothered me now.

He took my hand, leading me the way a father led a child who had tripped. And while I had tripped, I was not a child. In one breath he extolled my virtues as a researcher, urging me to explain what I knew. In the next, he dismissed me. While this wasn't something I had noticed earlier, my intoxication seemed to enlighten me. I'm sure it wouldn't make me a better researcher, but socially, it got my gears going and helped me see Gregorio's charm for what it most likely was, a facet of his suave personality and one that wouldn't mesh well with mine.

In my head, I compared him to Luke. The physical differences were slight if I didn't count the fact that one was mer and one was human. Hard, lean bodies and chiseled features were things they shared. However, the differences in their personalities, as I knew them at least, were great. Gregorio's conversational grace was exactly what an ambassador, or his assistant, needed. He embodied the ability to speak with diplomacy and courtesy.

Luke may have the same talents, but he looked to be more comfortable, less formal. While self- aware, he didn't look to be self-conscious or anxious. The way he addressed his crew showed that. And Luke had a bit of a drawl, not an accent, but a slower manner of speaking than Gregorio.

At that point, upon recognizing Gregorio as less than my ideal, I figured it was time to see him to the door.

"Look, Gregorio, I'm happy to tell you anything you want to know about my research, the trench, and the light, but not tonight. Come by the lab and I can explain. But I think I let things go a bit too far tonight," I tried to explain, removing his hands from my shoulders and turning toward the door.

"Too far? Really?" he asked. "I don't see it that way. I think we've just started."

He followed me to the open door, but he didn't leave.

"It's still early, Anya. And there is no need to rush to the lab tomorrow if I'm already here to talk to."

"Well, that's not exactly my plan. I appreciate you seeing me home, but I think I made a mistake. Why don't we just remember the night without any of that, alright?"

"You can try to forget, but I'm sure you won't be able to. I'll see you tomorrow." He leaned down, kissed my forehead, and waited just outside the door while I closed it, locked it, and turned out the porch light. I needed him to understand, and while I felt rude, having him feel I was playing hard to get wasn't an appetizing option.

Between the rum and the time spent thinking about the gorgeous human, I apparently jumped the gun and kissed the first hunk mer I came across. Not my finest moment, but by far not my worst. I was too tired to berate myself anyway. Besides, I had things to do, and dreaming about Luke was the first on the list.

TEN : LUKE

THE BOAT DRIFTED closer to the island, but not close enough for us to gain any help.

"You'd think someone would see us," Amir said. "If we see buildings, they must see us. Someone has to be out fishing at least."

"We're on the wrong side. I bet there's a harbor or something on the other side," Brandon acknowledged.

Looking over the island, Amir added, "Yeah, there must be an easier approach than that rock coast over there."

I knew they were right. No one would purposefully use a coastline covered in rock as an exit point when there was most likely a bay and port on the other side of the island. But I also figured someone would come to our side of the island at some point.

Kate interrupted my logic with her own. "Even if they disembark from a harbor, there must be fish on this side of the island. Look at the dolphin pod."

"Dolphin mean fish," Lucy joined. "But those are acting a little weird."

She was right. The dolphin didn't appear to be hunting. There was no rounding or trapping fish in their circle in order to herd them. No, it was obvious that the animals were playing, not prepping for a meal. But their play was odd, too. These animals were the right size, but all we saw were their tails breach the surface. The color seemed off, too. I chalked it up to the dawning light before sunrise. I refused to consider it may be mermaids. I couldn't jump to that conclusion for every oddity the ocean offered.

I agreed with Lucy, but brought up another concern. "There must be something keeping the locals from this side. Is there a reef, Norton?"

"Your guess is as good as mine, man. I can't find the damn island, forget a harbor or reef," the captain answered.

Norton had spent the long night with flashlights and maps, working to chart the course and keep the boat from straying too far. What he didn't see, however, was the island. The island right in front of us was nowhere on the maps.

A reef would invite fish and dolphin, but keep strangers at bay. It could offer safety to the island dwellers, at least if the ocean depths remained shallow overhead. A reef would also make it impossible for their boats. Of course, all of that depended on whether there were island dwellers and boats.

Figuring I could swim for help if we drifted a bit closer, I settled in again. The team theorized about the balls of light, settling on the premise of electrical magnetic pulses associated with random tectonic plate shifts. Two potential problems with two probable solutions. To me, that was as good as no problems at all.

As day began to break, the sun filled the sky with pink light. The red that crossed the sky after the storm predicted a beautiful day for sailors and the prediction was taking shape. The water danced rather than rollicked, and the boat gently rolled with the small waves drawing it closer to the island. The dolphins had since swum away and we dozed. The *Sea Star* drifted a few miles closer to the island, close enough that I could swim the distance without a problem.

"Gonna go for it, Luke?" Lucy posed the question already knowing the answer.

"Yep. No reason we should sit and wait. I'll just go find someone and head back out."

"Okay," she answered. "Be careful. It looks like a good five miles or so now. We've been drifting closer at least."

"I'm set. No worries, Luce. No worries."

She nodded towards me before burying her head in a book. Not one to worry, Lucy trusted me and got back to her own business. Taking her lack of interest as authorization, her version at least, I changed into a swimsuit and rash guard, and set out.

Jumping into the water freed me of my earlier anxiety. After acclimating, feeling the water caress my body, I started long, broad strokes towards the island. I crossed a third of the distance quickly. At that point, I dove below the surface, taking time to recognize various fish and coral. The water reached depths I hadn't expected that close to the shore.

Resurfacing, I saw Amir on deck of the boat. He waved, ensuring me that they were looking out for me, literally. I waved back and dove again. I noticed a mast stretching up from the ocean floor. A shipwreck? Figuring

I guessed correctly, I moved forward rather than venturing further down. It was covered with algae and not easy to make out. I could come back and look later, and I would. Now I needed to reach the island and find someone to tow the *Sea Star* in for repair.

The tide moved out and I drifted on the waves for a minute. I noticed the palm fronds sway in the tropical breeze which swirled through the vegetation on the beach beyond the rocks. Extending from the beach, the rocks seemed to sink into the carpet of sand. They prohibited any approach on that side, just as the crew suspected.

"That explains the shipwreck," I figured. "Not much could cross that wreath of rock."

The coral barrier also explained why we hadn't seen a boat that morning. It shrouded the island, forming a protective semicircle that reached half a mile from the shore. As the water level dropped, the reef stood far taller than I imagined. Parts reached out of the water, and at low tide the rocks formed small mountains covered with coral landscaping. Wishing I could enjoy a dive among the structures, I reluctantly navigated around the spires and toward the rock-strewn beach. The waves picked up near the barrier and tossed me towards a large rock. I powered through the wave, pushed against the forceful wall of water breaking across the ridge. The next wave hit harder though, and I dove under to avoid a push into the rock rampart. Still, coral gouged my side as I rolled through the water. The burning sensation stopped me. I grabbed the fresh cut, watching a red ribbon float through the water. Bobbing back to the surface, I caught my breath, hand at my side. Trying to move beyond the barrier, I reached through the saltwater with one arm feeling the gash burn with every stroke.

Something nudged my foot. Hard. I worked through the water with one arm, kicking in smooth strokes. The second nudge shook me and the third caused panic. I looked down noticing a large shadow moving below. Another shadow came in from the right and my panic deepened. Tiger sharks weren't known for swimming away from a waiting meal. My cut, while superficial, continued to bleed. The sharks continued to circle, swiping me as I swam closer to the beach. I felt the tip of a dorsal fin brush my stomach and saw the black eyes move past.

Should I kick at the closest predator, hoping to connect with the snout and injure it? Should I dive to swim faster? I refused both options figuring a kick through the water wouldn't be hard or fast enough to matter. If I dove, I may move faster, but I'd also lessen the one advantage I had. The sharks may not come up to the surface for me, and I needed air.

Without another option, I swam forward as quickly as I could. I swam faster than some men who had the use of two arms, but the sharks continued to circle. Closing the distance, one shark raced towards me, breaching the surface, its mouth open and ready.

Suddenly, amid my concerns and decisions, a pulse oscillated through the water and the sharks turned. Without looking towards me, they glided away, leaving me alone. I looked around. Only one thing caused a turn and burn in the shark world, a bigger threat. If a larger predator coiled through the sea at that moment, I didn't want to know.

As I contemplated what else could be in the reef, lurking, a new shadow emerged beneath me. It was long, lean, and gave off a metallic green cast rather than the dull gray of the sharks. It moved elegantly as its tail swirled in the current. I looked harder and noticed more. Hair. Arms. It swam towards me. The glow from the tail wasn't a glow exactly, but a shimmer, a shine. The tail shown with glints of green and blue. I knew when the sunshine caught the scales that it was her. I wouldn't forget the color of her scales, how they matched her eyes.

And now I was hurt and possibly hallucinating mermaids.

But I knew different. Hallucinations weren't the issue. She existed. She swam the seas with dolphins and controlled sharks. I saw her not once, but twice, and I knew she existed.

ELEVEN: ANYA

HE SPOTTED ME and stopped swimming. He hung there looking around as I rolled over in the water and looked up at him. He must have seen me when I approached his ship a day ago. He had probably seen me swimming with Phoebe beyond the reef earlier that morning, too.

In a moment of awareness, I saw him come to terms with sudden recognition. He knew I sent the sharks away. The thoughts crossed his face, and he realized there could be no other reason he wasn't chum at the moment.

I caught sight of his cut, thought a moment, and swam away. He floated there, treading water and wondering what would happen next. At that point, his face conveyed the pain in his side. I watched an intense sting replace what I knew of the original burning sensation of a coral abrasion, and the open wound spilled into the ocean at a steady pace.

Conceivably, I had underestimated the severity of the cut. Maybe the coral cut deeper than I thought. The blood clouded the water surrounding him, and now the problem remained of how to take the injured man across the reef without doing further damage. We still needed to cross at least two miles and climb a rocky beach. Or did we?

Before he had time to contemplate any other option, I approached him from below. I swam up to him slowly, and he did nothing. He didn't dive to meet me or attempt to swim away. He hung vertically in the water, waiting.

He must have felt me before he could clearly see me. The water shifted as I neared, my physicality changing the flow of the ocean around me. He knew I was there, but he didn't dive below. Was he afraid? Too hurt to move? Instead, he stayed still, moving as little as possible, allowing my approach, and keeping the blood loss at a minimum.

I moved below him and then up, along his body, until my head emerged from the inky blue water and he stared into my eyes. He let out a fast gasp and quickly sank below the surface.

I dove down and drew him up, my arms across his chest. We reached the surface and he breathed deeply, taking as much air into his lungs as he could and wincing in pain.

He asked questions, but I said nothing. I merely palpated the injured area ensuring the condition of his ribs. Finding him in one piece, I wrapped my arms around him from behind to keep him afloat and allow him to rest. Then I explained.

"You have questions. I understand. But for now, trust me."

His face conveyed his obvious confusion and surprise. Prepared for both, I responded. "I promise to explain after. I can only keep the sharks away for so long, and you're bleeding. I can't control all of the ocean's predators, so we need to go."

Luke nodded in agreement, ready to be on land and wondering how I could get him there.

"We're going to swim to that cave," I announced, pointing to the southeast end of the island, away from the jetty, and leaving no room for his refusal. "It looks like a big rock, but there is a cave. It has an air chamber, so you'll be fine once we get there."

I gave him exactly one minute to prepare, then I swam with him the same way lifeguards swim with victims. Knowing what happened when victims fought, he remained placid. We cut through the surf quickly and silently. I carved our path with strong strokes, my fluid movements working against waves and wind. We crossed the open water in minutes.

As we approached the rock, I quickly explained that we needed to swim under water to the cave opening.

"The entrance is almost at the sea floor. You'll need to hold your breath for more than three minutes," I instructed. "Can you do that?"

Luke nodded, thankful for his swimming habit and questioning the depth of the bay if it took me three minutes to enter the cave.

I counted to three before we plunged below the surface and I towed him to the hollow. I moved a group of small rocks and a few larger ones without trouble. Turning to check on him occasionally, I felt reassured by his thumbs up signs. We entered the cave slowly. Luke didn't know what I looked for as I searched the cavern, but my apprehension was obvious.

Eventually satisfied, I brought him through the opening. We surged to the surface once inside and Luke repeatedly swallowed air, feeding his lungs. He noticed the water, compressed and still flowing, churned violently. He also noticed no way out.

"How, how are we getting out of here?" he asked.

"This cave is one in a sequence. We move through three altogether before we get to the island. Each gets larger and is filled with more air than the one before. It allows my tail and gills a chance to transition for land. The entrances are near the bottom just like this one. Ready?"

He gulped air and felt me pull him under again. We entered the second cave and as promised, it held more air than the last. Our rest there equaled a fraction of the time spent in the first cave, and we dove for the third opening.

The third held only a few feet of water and Luke noticed the vestiges of my tail, the scales joining my legs, vanish. They transformed from the shining surface of my fin to the smooth, tan skin of my legs. The scales dissolved, almost blending into each other and paling quickly. My gills did the same, but while my tail left no visible trace behind, my gills remained, although closed. A soft, white line reminiscent of a scar lingered.

With my legs fully formed, we exited the cave and walked onto a sand beach. The rock formations behind us blocked what he had seen as the only entrance to the island. The beach where we stood appeared tropical and lush, and probably the opposite of what the crew noticed from the boat. With the rocky shoreline behind us, I led him to a fallen palm and forced him to sit. While it seemed he wouldn't have asked for the rest, he appreciated it all the same.

"Are you well?" I asked, my concern apparent on my face and in my voice.

"I'm not worse," he answered. "But I do have more questions."

"I figured you would. We can rest here a minute, but then we need to get you cleaned up. I'll answer what I can then."

"Can I at least know your name?" he quizzed.

"Oh, yes. That is time we can spare," I said with a smile. "I'm Anya, and you are?" I figured there was no reason to let him know I already had that information. Best we start on even ground, so to speak.

"Luke. Luke McAllister. My friends are on the ship about five miles past the reef. Our boat, it's a research vessel, needs fixing, so I tried to swim in for help."

"Well, Luke." I smiled, disarming him somewhat. "I have friends who can help with that. But rest a minute first. I'm just going over there to put on some clothes."

He nodded, in no shape to argue with me about anything, an injured stranger on an unmapped island. I walked a few feet away and reached for a guava hanging

75

ripe and full on a low branch. He watched me, nude and unashamed, stretch my legs. He noticed the neat footprints I left in the sand. Returning to him, I handed him my harvest and encouraged him to begin eating.

"You could use the water," I mentioned. "And this one is ripe and sweet. You'll love it."

He bit into the plump, green fruit. Juice dripped from his chin, and he wiped at it with the back of his hand. I noticed him flinch in pain after raising his arm and encouraged him to finish the snack before putting on my sundress.

"We need to clean out that gash. Coral cuts can harbor bacteria. They're quick to get infected, you know."

"Okay, but where. Is there a doctor close?"

I gestured to the tree line and the small path that led to a clapboard house with a red roof. We walked through the vegetation and into the house. Lualla, an older mermaid, stood inside and looked up in surprise. Her eyes went straight to Luke.

"Alavay. And who is this, Anya?" Lualla asked coolly.

I remained stoic, not acknowledging her discomfort. "This is Luke. His boat had some trouble and he needs help," I retorted unapologetically.

"Excuse us please. Anya, a moment." Lualla walked away from Luke, and not wanting to meet her gaze, I followed.

In a hushed tone, Lualla asked, "And who is this?"

"He's a researcher, and his boat had some trouble out past the reef," I said, trying to sound confident. "He was swimming in for help and had an issue with the sharks."

"And what do you plan to do with him?" her tone sounding more clipped as she spoke.

There was plenty I considered doing, but I didn't mention that to Lualla.

"I planned to send a boat out to help his crew, and maybe --". This is where Lualla began to lose her patience.

"You plan to do what? This is not acceptable, Anya, and you of all mer should know better."

"But he's researching the trench. The same trench that I'm working with right now. The energy source." I could hear myself pleading with her to understand.

"Does Nishan know? Or Jinsen?"

"No one knows but you, right now. And I think your attitude toward the human could really help me smooth things over with the rest."

"I don't like this, Anya. I think it's a mistake."

"I know and I understand, but please, please help me out. If you accept him and his crew, at least for now, others will too."

Lualla had influence with the tribe due not only to her age but to reserved demeanor and practicality. She was a lovely mer with a kind heart and a grandmotherly attitude toward most of us.

"How many of them are coming?" she asked already planning for their housing needs.

"I think the team is six in all, including Luke."

"Six humans. All running around the island during the festival? This will be a hard sell, Anya. Get ready to be convincing," she said. "Use the main guest house, I suppose."

Surprised by her willingness to offer up such a beautiful cottage to the crew, I asked, "Are you sure? What if we have embassy visitors?"

"We shouldn't. Everyone coming here is here, we can hope," she said nodding towards Luke.

She turned to Luke, showing me the conversation was over. I followed.

"Welcome, Luke," she said brightly. "Let's get him set up." Suddenly she was smiles and warmth.

"Thanks, Lualla. I'll head into the other room. I need some med supplies. You're in good hands Luke. Just call when he's all set," and I slipped away to another room, leaving Luke with the soft-spoken mermaid.

Lualla reached for a soft cotton t-shirt, a pair of cargo shorts, and leather flip-flop sandals.

"Here you go, dear. There is a changing room in there, but don't put the shirt on until you have that cut looked at."

He moved to the curtained alcove and changed from his wet swimsuit into the dry clothing, thankful for the opportunity. Emerging from the changing room, he looked around for me. I had changed out of the sand-covered dress and came around the corner wearing a tank top and skirt, my hair pulled into a loose bun on the top of my head.

"You look like those girls who made my head swim in college. You're all long, golden legs and arms and sun-streaked hair," he accidentally said aloud. Immediately blushing, he looked around embarrassed.

I smiled, letting myself be excited by his appreciation. That one moment made it clear that last night and Gregorio were a mistake. I wanted my head to swim because of Luke's compliment, not too many glasses of rum punch.

"You're the best, Lualla," I called back over my shoulder, taking Luke's hand and leading him outside. "Now let's get your cut fixed up."

TWELVE: LUKE

THE CREW OF the *Sea Star* reached Orotava by fishing boat.

As the crew disembarked the rescue vessel, the uneven pier creaked and the group worked to regain their land legs. Each held a few bags, except Amir who struggled under the computers and other equipment we used often. The dock felt longer under the hot island sun and heavy-handed humidity.

I walked out to meet my friends. My newly stitched and bandaged side hobbled me enough to strain my gait. Ambling towards them, I called out with a smile, "Nice of you to show up. Been waiting a while."

"Hey, man. Whatcha got there?" Brandon asked, pointing towards my side.

"Oh, just a few stitches. Caught my side on coral. Burns like a son-of-a-gun."

"That'd be 32 stitches," Anya added, coming up behind me.

The crew stared at the beautiful blond.

"Oh, this is Anya," I said, motioning to the woman. "Her friends brought you in. And she brought me in."

"You didn't need me. You were fine, if bloody and broken doesn't bother you," she joked.

The group offered their thanks and Anya rewarded them with warm smiles and welcomes. Their rescuers waved their goodbyes and returned to their fishing, leaving us with Anya and our baggage.

"Luke said you might bring your equipment. We have a spot for all of you in the village, and Javier will head out to check on your boat if that's alright."

Norton spoke up. "That'd be fine, miss. I'll head out with him whenever he's ready. But I'd love to find some food first if that's an option."

"You must be Norton. Luke told me you wouldn't allow anyone on your boat without you."

"Yes, ma'am. She's my girl," he explained.

"That's just fine. Javier will appreciate that. And we can find you some food right now. The Sword and Dagger has the best spread on the island."

"The Sword and Dagger?" Lucy questioned.

"Orotava's best tavern," Anya announced with a grand smile. "My uncle runs it. The guest house, the one we've set up for you, is just behind it."

Kate's interest peaked. "A guest house? Already? How long have you been on the island, Luke?"

"Oh, just enough time to get cleaned up. Anya works quick. She knows everyone and they were all eager to help out."

With a smile, Anya grabbed one of the boxes Amir carried. I attempted to grab one, but my stitches made it impossible. We followed her down the pier and into the quaint, cobblestoned village. The narrow streets resembled paths rather than roads and people milled about. Small buildings grouped together with businesses and cottages mixed throughout.

Anya led us to the guest house first, opening the door to the white-sided bungalow. Each of us entered the charming home with eyes wide. After setting her bags in the front room, Lucy walked straight through the cottage to the back porch.

"Get out here, guys," she called. "Seriously, get out here!"

We jostled to get out back, haphazardly making it through the double French door to the porch. There we found a wide, covered porch complete with rocking chairs and a porch swing. The view sucked us in. Lucy gestured to the marina spotted with boats of all sizes from dinghies to catamarans.

"There's a dolphin pod," she exclaimed pointing with excitement.

"We have a few native pods," Anya offered. "They come to and from the bay. It's like their home base. Some even have names."

Lucy shrieked with delight. "I can see them every day?"

"Yep, they'll be here throughout the day. You'll get to know them if you stick around a while."

Not needing to hear any more, Lucy took off to the beach towards the pod.

"She'll be fine, right?" Kate asked, concerned for the younger woman.

"Oh, there's nothing here that'd hurt her," Anya confirmed. "She's absolutely safe. As long as she can swim that is," she added with a sweet smile. .

Turning to me, she suggested, "Perhaps your friends would like to rest or eat."

Norton perked up suddenly. Not interested in dolphins or views, he laughed. "That's exactly what I'd like to do. I don't know about the rest of you. Hell, for that matter, I don't care."

"Perfect. You all get settled, unpacked, washed up, whatever you need. I'll be back in about an hour and give you a tour. If you need anything in the meantime, you should find it inside."

With that, Anya saw herself out, leaving us on the porch together.

Brandon finally tore his eyes off the door the graceful woman exited. "Wow!" he breathed. "Who is she?"

"Anya? I told you, she met me on the rocks at the jetty. Said she'd seen me swimming and figured I could use some help."

I'd have to remember that was now our story and fill her in on it later, just in case. I wasn't about to explain that I'd been rescued by a shark-controlling mermaid who made a hell of a surgeon.

"That's weird. We didn't see anyone meet you."

"Oh, well, she met me on the far side, on the rocks. You probably wouldn't see her there."

"I guess not," Brandon agreed, too captivated to think it through more thoroughly.

"So, what's her story?" Amir chimed in. "Pretty girl. Unmapped island. Kinda mysterious."

I conceded. "The unmapped island is definitely mysterious. I haven't had a chance to ask much about it yet. Maybe it's just missing from our map. I mean you saw the infrastructure."

"Haven't had a chance?" Kate questioned.

"I wasn't about to interrogate her as she stitched me up. 'Hey, thanks for the help and all, but why don't you guys show up on a map?' Not exactly subtle."

Kate agreed. "No, it's not subtle. But it would make sense. I mean didn't you ask her anything?"

"Yea, I asked things. Mostly stuff like 'What's your name? Where are we? Where are we going? Hey, do you know how to do that?' You know, stuff I found important."

Brandon interrupted, "Not exactly what I'd find important, man. More like 'Are you single?'"

Shaking her head, Kate redirected the conversation. "And did she answer any of those questions?"

"Yes, Kate," I sniped back at her defensively. "She did. The island is Orotava, we were headed to her cottage, and she stitched up her brothers plenty of times. That was good enough for me."

"Well, as long as you did your research," Kate scoffed and walked inside.

I motioned for the guys to hang on a second. I ran back to the kitchen and returned with four beers. One thing I did learn was that the Orotavans were hospitable.

"Now we can talk," Amir agreed, grabbing a bottle from my hand and taking a long swig.

THIRTEEN: ANYA

I SPENT MY hour at the lab, looking into the readings from the night before. Just as I suspected, the research vessel found itself caught in tectonic pulses. The oscillations fried their systems and left them without a GPS and without an engine.

The light began showing up about a year ago, but last night was the first time it left the sea. Not only that, but it was the first time a non-Obthalusian had dealt with any of it. That meant the energy wasn't tribally specific as I once hypothesized. If it affected anyone, I had plenty of new questions to research.

I had no way to prove or disprove the hypothesis until now. But considering the energy interfered with a boat without an Obthalusian passenger meant it wasn't focused on anything specific about the island or the tribe. This also meant that if we could reproduce the result, potentially anyone else would be able to do the same. And that meant the one hope we had that the energy could only be controlled by those from the Obthaluse tribe vanished.

Now I had a new reason to dive into my research and Luke, a new distraction, to keep me from it. Beyond my fascination with the gorgeous man, there were humans on the island. I had to figure a way to handle my tribe's reaction. No one in the tribe would be happy with the interference, but Nishan would be devastated. The issue that they were on the island could shake him quickly. My association with them, my being the reason they were on the island, promised to send him reeling.

My father never trusted humans, and he blamed them for my mother's death. And there was no way he would settle into the idea of me being associated with them.

⌁

I RETURNED TO the guest house a little more than an hour later, ready to get the crew some food and introduce them around the island. I didn't have a plan of how I'd handle the tribe's reactions to them, but I'd figure it out as we went.

Luke and the guys finished their beers and called to Lucy who was still on the beach. Kate joined us outside, fresh from the shower and toweling her wet hair. We stood beside each other looking like matching bookends. However, it seemed our faces held a distinct difference. I smiled, happy to meet these interesting humans so dedicated to studying our ocean even if their presence proved detrimental to me. However, Kate showed no expression. Her face remained void of any emotion as though she were playing poker. This skepticism made it obvious she still questioned my agenda and situation. I wondered if my concerns came across as clearly too.

"I knocked, but I figured you were all out here," I said. "Are you ready to see the island or do you want to eat first?"

Since they had snacked on what they found in the kitchen, they agreed to a tour.

Together, we set out to explore Orotava. I led them away from the pier they'd seen earlier and towards the center of town.

"So where are we?" Kate asked.

"Orotava," I answered.

"And what is Orotava?" Kate insisted, obviously frustrated with the lack of detail I offered.

"My family founded the island hundreds of years ago. We sit at about 28 longitude and -68 latitude, in the middle of the Atlantic. Southwest of Devil's Isle, east of Florida, and Northwest of Puerto Rico."

Brandon perked up. "Devil's Isle? Bermuda? That means we're smack dab in the middle of the Triangle?"

I nodded.

"That's it. Explains everything," Norton added. "It's the damn triangle."

"It explains nothing," Kate snapped. Ever the scientist, she refused to brush things off and blame them on superstition. "Well, unless you're willing to believe that geography can stop a boat and turn off GPS," she groaned.

Amir, not as easily swayed to disbelief, argued. "That's exactly what I believe. Why not, Kate? There's plenty of electromagnetic energy floating around. Why not a spot with enough to throw off a GPS?"

I escorted the researchers past stores and homes. Small buildings of coquina brick or graying wood siding stood on both sides of the path mixing with the lush vegetation. Palms and elephant ear plants spread their large green leaves. Hibiscus bushes flounced their red and yellow blossoms while clematis climbed and wound their way in and out of other plants. Luke looked around the paradise. His face showed wonder at how his mundane research voyage turned surreal.

"What's that, over there, with the dish on the roof?" Kate asked, finally over her snit about the Bermuda Triangle.

"Oh, that's our research facility. We have a few folks looking into the native flora, others studying the dolphin pods. It's a universal space. Those interested are welcome to the equipment," I explained. "I do a little research there when I have time."

Excitement reached Kate's eyes. "Those interested? Even us?" she asked.

"Sure. I don't see it being a problem."

"Well, you won over Kate," Brandon piped in. "And Lucy was set when she saw the pod. Just us now, Anya." He gestured to himself and the three other men.

Norton spoke up. "Speak for yourself, kid. Beer and beach and someone to help work on the *Sea Star*. What else do I need?"

"Okay, fine. Just three of us now."

I smiled and turned the group around, moving back towards the guest house, all the while wondering if I'd won over Luke yet. I tried to put the thought out of my mind, but it remained.

The smell of frying fish lead us straight to the doors of the Sword and Dagger. The tavern sat off the path overlooking the inlet. It had no glass in the window openings allowing the warm breeze to blow through the pub. The antique, carved bar and round pedestal tables shared the same nautical engravings of anchors and compasses. The bar, however, included a scene across the front of a mermaid leading a pirate ship away from a giant octopus. Wide wood planks covered the floors and walls and the tavern resembled the interior of a clipper ship.

"Alavay, Anya," the older man behind the bar called. "Company, eh?"

"Alavay. These are the folks whose ship broke down outside the reef. Luke, Norton, Brandon, Kate, Amir, and Lucy," I introduced, pointing to each. "And this is my Uncle Rowan."

"Nice place you got here," Norton added. "Whatcha got on tap?"

"Three taps, no bottles unless you count the rum," Rowan explained. "Dark, light, and amber. What'll you have?"

Norton smiled and grabbed a stool at the bar. "This is my kind of place. I'll take a light and whatever you've got frying in the back. Smells great."

"It's cod. And it's good."

"Cod?" Brandon questioned. "How far away do you have to go to get cod?"

"It's closer than you'd think," Rowan offered, not actually explaining how he got hold of a northern Atlantic fish. It would take ships weeks to reach cod fishing ground, fish, and return. But mermaids move much faster and have unsurpassed fishing skills. "Anyone else interested?"

Everyone decided to follow Norton's lead. Rowan drew the beers and went to the back, calling to me over his shoulder. "Uh, Anya, come help if you would."

I knew what that meant. I was in trouble.

Heading to the small kitchen, I hung my head anticipating the lecture to come.

"I know what you're going to say," I started.

"Do you? Do you know?" Rowan barked back. "If you know, why don't you tell me?"

"You're going to tell me that I brought a group of humans into your bar, a group I know nothing about, and I did it during the festival on top of all of it. And you're going to ask me if I've told Nishan about them yet. And when I say no, you're going to turn red and walk away."

"Close," he said shaking his head. "Very close, but wrong. I know you haven't told your father. Your father has plenty of other people telling him about this, and he doesn't need you to do it. He did ask me to watch you, though. He knew you wouldn't stay away from the boat. Granted, I think it was the research he figured you'd be after, not the researcher."

How did he know how I felt about Luke? Was it that obvious? Shocked, I stumbled to regain my composure.

"He knows? Who is telling him things?" Dumbfounded, I couldn't begin to guess who else had knowledge of the crew and the time to get word to my father.

"You're buddy Greg has a big mouth, young lady. That tends to be the case when a man's pride is hurt."

"What are you talking about?"

"Really? Anya, you're smarter than that. Greg ran to Nishan when he realized you have eyes for that sailor in there." He motioned to the barroom. "We can talk about this later. I have people to feed."

Handing me two plates, he put the rest on a tray and walked through the swinging door to the bar. Reluctantly, I followed, carrying plates heavy with fried fish and potatoes, golden and crisp. The smell alone had the team anxiously picking up forks.

I knew there was something about Gregorio that hadn't set well with me, but I never figured it would be his willingness to tattle on me to my father.

"This is amazing," Lucy announced through a mouth full of flaky fish.

Kate nodded in agreement, not willing to stop eating to comment. The guys slowed enough to order another round of beers. I, however, ate while explaining more about Orotava.

"The island isn't very big," I noted. "We figure that's why we aren't on most maps. Some of them have us, but we're listed as unpopulated. I guess folks figure no one would want to live on such a small piece of land. Or maybe it's just because there are so many barriers to the island."

Rowan looked at the researchers, trying to read their take on that news.

Kate was the first to respond. "So cartographers, topographers for that matter, just overlook the island?"

"It's easier than you'd think," Rowan added as he dried glasses and put them away. "It isn't like there is much out here to attract them. No unknown species have been attributed here. No neighboring islands really. You'd have to aim for Orotava to pay attention."

"Then there's the fact that our governor of sorts paid off a huge map-making company in Boston to keep us uncharted over 250 years ago," I added.

Luke finished a swig of beer and looked admiringly at his crew. "I thought I saw a wreck when I was swimming in this morning. How many downed ships do you deal with?"

"You got caught in the storm last night I'm guessing. Hell of a storm," Rowan added.

"Luke decided to swim in since no one was reef-side today. They weren't sure when someone would see their boat," I said.

Rowan seemed surprised. "Swam the reef, did ya? Not too many attempt that."

Luke was nonchalant, but he seemed a bit on edge. "I can see why. Hell of a reef to come up against. It bit me pretty hard." He put his hand to his bandaged side.

"Then you must've seen the *Vengeful Dane*," Rowan continued. "She's has been there a long time. I don't much think about her anymore."

"How long has she been there?" Brandon inquired.

"Give or take 200 years."

"Well she's well preserved then," Luke added. "I'd have expected far less wood left."

Rowan brightened at the discussion. He loved that ship. "We've done a lot to keep her that way."

"Luke, we should dive the ship. That's alright, isn't it, Rowan?" Brandon asked, finishing his pint and motioning for another.

"Sure. Just watch the sharks. They circle that reef. Good eating for them even without divers floating about."

The team spent the afternoon in the tavern, talking with me and Rowan and meeting the few locals who came in for a drink or dinner.

As we rose to leave, Gregorio walked in.

"Alavay, Anya. I've been looking for you," Gregorio started as he walked across the room.

"Oh, I'm sorry," I began. "Luke and his friends needed some help. I didn't realize we had plans."

"Oh, are you all from the boat beyond the reef?" he asked. Not waiting for an answer, he continued, "No problem. I knew you wouldn't leave me waiting without a good reason."

"But I didn't leave you waiting," I added in my own defense.

"Well, you did tell me to come by the lab today. I figured if I went by, you'd be there. Obviously I was wrong. You had other things to do."

He leaned over and kissed my cheek delicately. I felt myself flush with the awkward attention. However, instead of acknowledging my discomfort, I made introductions to the group. Finishing our food, we said good byes to Gregorio and Rowan.

"Goodnight, all. I trust you'll have a pleasant night," Gregorio said to the team. "Anya, will we meet tomorrow?"

"Oh, well, I'll be in the lab most of the day. I suppose if you want to come by I could make time for you," I said reluctantly.

"I'd appreciate that. Even a sliver of her time is worth a wait. Don't you agree, Luke?"

Catching him off guard, Luke took a long look at me and answered Gregorio, "Very true, Greg. Very true."

"It's Gregorio," he commented in a sharp tone. "Anya, I'll be down to the lab then."

Nodding in agreement, I kissed Rowan on the cheek and headed out with the team.

The sun hung low over the water by the time we left and headed towards the guest house. Norton made plans to meet with my friends and work on the *Sea Star* the next day, and the team had nothing to do other than sit on the porch and discuss their options and the island.

While they all knew their research needed to continue, the boat became their first priority. With the plan for repairs made, Kate suggested they look into the island's research and communication facilities. After all, her family needed to know her whereabouts. Brandon's concern lie in the downed ship and the chance to excavate a bit. Norton focused on the boat, as expected, and Lucy had the dolphins to obsess over. That left Luke and Amir, the wild cards. Amir figured he'd join one of the others in their ventures, but Luke wasn't so quick to commit to anything. Other than setting up a time for us to meet alone the next day, Luke had no need for plans. And what I hoped to do would lend itself best to time alone with him as well.

FOURTEEN: LUKE

THE MORNING AFTER we landed in Orotava, Kate and Norton took off for their personal endeavors with most of our equipment before the rest of us woke. Lucy set out for the marina after scrounging up something to eat and Brandon and Amir headed to the beach. By the time I entered the kitchen, it sat vacant and thoroughly rummaged. I found a stray bagel on the counter and some coffee left in the pot. Grabbing both, I ventured onto the porch.

My head swam with the details of the past two days. The balls of light. The joint fainting spell. The reef. The sharks. The mermaid. I'd seen a mermaid, twice, and then she turned human and stitched me up. I'd eaten dinner with her and learned about her life. Anya rescued me, she met my crew, and she'd shown us around the island. But I still had so many questions for her. Did she consider the cottage her home or did she live in the sea? Why did the tribe hold land? In which environment was she more comfortable? Where did she truly feel alive?

The new issue was that I'd seen her transform and watched the scales give way to smooth skin. Seeing her naked in human form was enough to distract me from her being a mermaid, at least for a minute.

A knock at the door startled me from my internal interrogation. I opened it and took in the sight of Anya almost glowing in the morning sun.

"Come in," I said as I finally found words. "Good morning."

I turned to welcome her in and tripped over the corner of the throw rug.

"Good morning. I hope it isn't too early," she returned, snickering a little at my stupor. "I didn't want to wake anyone. You all had quite a day yesterday."

"Oh, no, not at all. I'm the only one here, though. Hope that's alright."

"Great. I mean I was hoping to talk to you. I set Norton up with Javier, and Maya told me Kate was down at the research lab early."

"That's our Kate. She wanted to get a hold of her son most of all, but research is her second love. You're lucky she waited until morning."

"A son?" Anya cooed. I could see the twinkle in her eye at the mention of a child. "No wonder she was anxious."

"The rest are at the beach, I'm sure. We won't be able to drag Lucy along when we decide to leave if the pods are still here."

"I saw them as I walked up. They're at the marina. Lucy and Amir were fishing, and it looked like Brandon was sunbathing."

I didn't mean to, but I laughed at the vision of my vain and muscle-bound friend laid out on the towel.

"Sounds like Brando. I guess everyone's accounted for then. That gives us time to talk."

"Well, first I wanted to check your bandage."

Hesitating a bit, I removed my shirt and raised my arm, allowing her a clear view of the bandage. Suddenly I felt uncomfortable in this relaxed environment. Something between us had shifted and I was uneasy having her touch me.

"We should probably change it. I'd hate for the wound to get infected, and you never know with coral cuts."

As she removed the bandage, her fingers traced my rib. She sent shocks through my body reminding me of the pulse in the ocean, the one that sent the sharks away. Her touch stirred me and fired off more questions.

"The stitches look good. They aren't red and they're holding well," she remarked with surprise. Her response concerned me a little. Astonishment wasn't something I wanted to hear in my surgeon's voice, after all. But I merely nodded and murmured agreement.

Anya bandaged me and stepped back avoiding any further contact with my bare skin. I found myself suddenly wishing that my thigh rather than my side had been gouged by the coral. Her touch would have done wonders there.

Trying to clear my head, I asked, "And what else did you want to discuss?"

I hoped she would broach the mermaid topic without prompting. Not knowing how to begin the conversation, I found myself relying on her again.

"Well, I'm sure you've noticed the island's unique aspects," she said.

"Unique aspects? Is that Orotavan for mermaids?"

The sarcasm dripping from my comment startled her. Seeing her reaction, I apologized quickly.

"Anya, I'm sorry. I just don't know what to make of all this. I saw you. From the boat. While I was on the boat I mean. You were swimming with something, or someone

I guess. And then in the lagoon. You made the sharks turn back. Now you're standing here, checking my bandage and the stitches you put in. I can't explain any of it." I shook my head and turned away from her in frustration.

"I don't know how to help you understand other than to just tell you outright." She breathed deeply and I found myself thinking about her gills.

"So, how much do you want to know?" she asked.

"How much? As much as you're willing to tell."

"Alright, that's fair."

Another deep breath and she dove into an explanation.

"This is Orotava. That part you already know. My family founded the island. Centuries before humans took to the seas, mer lived in almost every body of water and on a number of islands. Each tribe took a different section. The Obthaluse, that's my tribe, had the North American coast of the Atlantic and pieces of the Caribbean as well. Orotava was just one of the islands we inhabited."

"So there are more of you? Mermaids, I mean," I stammered. "In tribes? On islands or in the oceans?"

I couldn't seem to get the questions out quickly enough to satisfy my curiosity.

"Mer populate the waters across the globe. Most of the saltwater mer live in tribes even now. But lots of those in lakes and rivers live in smaller pods or alone. Tribes war and create alliances. We act much like humans, but we have far more territory to fight over than you do and we've been doing it a lot longer."

She sounded almost embarrassed of those facts as she continued.

"Our land holdings dwindle every year as humans claim more land for themselves, and we move further away, deeper into the seas. The Obthaluse have fewer than 20 islands to walk now, all small, and most unmapped. But many of those are collective islands."

"Collective islands? Like co-ops?" I asked. "So tribes mix on land?"

"Sometimes, yes. It's best if we all have our own space, but there isn't enough land for that anymore. We've learned to make do, and some tribes now inhabit human land."

"Seriously? Mermaids and humans and no one notices? Where? Where can that happen?"

"I bet you could figure it out if you thought hard enough." She laughed a bit, insisting. "Just think of the most ocean-centric places you can, and then limit the list to the vivid exceptions."

"Uh, ocean-centric places. Ok, so cities focusing on the beach. But what's a 'vivid exception'?"

I thought for a minute in silence and then lit up with the novelty of my guess. Laughing, I announced triumphantly, "Key West!"

"Yes, that's one. New Orleans is a big draw for mer, too."

"I could see that," I said thinking of my time in that great city. Who would guess they were dining with a mermaid when the actual humans were acting so strangely?

"Myrtle Beach is much smaller, but almost predominantly mer. And Provincetown, up in Rhode Island, that's our north most collective."

I contemplated the cities she mentioned. I'd been to all of them in my travels. But never, never had I thought I'd been working or dining or even dancing with mermaids.

"It's a lot to take in," I explained.

"I'm sure if I were faced with something I'd been told doesn't exist, I'd be a bit overwhelmed, too."

"Well, yea. There's that. Next you'll tell me you raise unicorns."

"No unicorns," she answered, adding sarcastically. "Unless you count narwhals. They are, after all, the unicorns of the sea."

Gorgeous, funny, and mysterious. I was in awe and smiling beyond my normal capacity. What had I swum into here?

"Fair enough. But I'm sure the island holds plenty of surprises you've yet to offer up," I teased.

She laughed, a tinkling laugh that got higher as she continued. It reminded me of a scale played on a flute, a pure, clear sound that cleared my head.

"We do have our share —"

"More than your share," I interrupted.

"True, more than our share. But you've hit the major ones already. There are a few left, but nothing that should throw you at this point."

"So the mermaid thing tops the list?"

"I'd say so," she agreed.

"So, how did you all get here? I mean you have electricity and Internet access."

"You have to remember, we've been here for hundreds of years."

"That's not surprising. Humans have been around for thousands," I countered.

"Yes, but I mean we, as individuals. Rowan is almost 200 years old."

I guffawed in surprise and retorted quickly, "How old are you?" with more shock in my voice than intended.

"Me? Guess," Anya challenged.

"This is the one thing they teach men not to do with human women. No guessing age or weight. Ever."

"Go ahead," she dared. "Give it a shot."

"Uh, maybe 45? 70? I mean in human years I'd say 25 or so."

"Good try. A valiant effort, but very, very wrong. More like 122." She smiled at her victory in having stumped me.

"Are you kidding me? That's not possible."

"It is possible, and yes, I'm 122. In fact, I'll be 123 in about two lunar cycles. Feel free to send a gift."

At that, I wondered what you buy a mermaid.

"So, where do you live?" I asked feeling rather naïve. I was staying on her island, but I wasn't sure that was her home.

"I spent most of my time in the ocean. Others, like Lualla, spend more time on land. Since she runs the largest store on Orotava, it makes sense that she walks more than she swims. But most are like me."

"So, why come on land at all?"

She smiled, understanding my confusion and interest. "We have land for the same reason humans have land. The more land a tribe or country has the more power it has. While it may not be true all the time, the mer are big on holdings. How much land, how much water, whether it is cold or warm, all of that makes a difference for us."

"And your family? Where are they? On the island or in the ocean?"

"I'm related to most of the island," she said. "You've already met my Uncle Rowan and Lualla is a cousin of some kind."

"What about your immediate family?"

"My mother died years ago. But my father is the tribal council leader. And my brothers are all over the place. Some are on land, others are swimming. Noran is an ambassador to the upper Atlantic. Paulo and Gratio work the Panama Canal, kind of like mer customs and immigration. Dartanan lives with his wife and children on the other side of the island where they run a small farm. Kellen is helping with research in the Great Barrier Reef. And my youngest brother, Korwin, is more of a free spirit."

"A free spirit?" I asked.

"He spends most of his time on the beach, smoking pot and drinking with his band" she confessed laughing.

"Well, good to know 'free spirit' means the same to humans as it does to mer. So that makes six brothers?"

"Yep, six. I was lucky number seven. My mother wanted a girl."

"And how did she die, Anya?" My voice softened as I knew I was asking a delicate question.

She turned away for a moment before she answered. "I'm not exactly sure. I was so young and my father doesn't like to talk about it. All I know is that it involved a human ship."

That left a lot of things to consider, and it explained why her father hated humans so much.

"But enough about me," she said more cheerfully. "What about you? What's your story?"

"It isn't much," I admitted. "And doesn't cover nearly the years yours does."

She laughed.

"I'm originally from Florida, just north of Miami. I have a sister who works in D.C. She's a lawyer for the

House of Representatives. My folks are both still in Florida and have me over for Sunday dinner when I'm around."

"What else? What about your research? Your team?"

"Well, I went to the University of Miami. That's where I met Kate. We were in classes together and competed for the same graduate awards."

"She beat you out, didn't she?" Anya joked.

"We split them 50/50," I said proudly. "The only reason she isn't the lead on this project is by choice. Her son, George, is seven and she claims not to have time to spend in the office researching. Says that's for dull, single guys."

"She thinks you're dull? Well that explains why you two aren't together."

"Not an option. She's more like family than dating material," I answered. "The rest kind of came together later. Lucy is my grad assistant right now. I'll be lost when she moves on. Brandon and Amir are a package deal. They've done all of their research together and really work as two sides of the same person. And Norton, he came with the boat."

We only stopped talking when we noticed Amir, Lucy, and Brandon walking up the beach to the cottage porch. The three happily recounted their morning. The guys spent some time casting off the pier and were exceptionally proud as they held up a string of snapper ready to be filleted and cooked.

Inviting Anya to join us for blackened fish sandwiches, a specialty of his, Brandon took the fish inside to prep them.

"I'd love to, really I would, but I have some other things to do before the day gets away from me," she explained before making her exit.

I watched her leave, knowing she was headed to meet the mer from yesterday. I also knew that I didn't care for that. I'd much rather she spent the afternoon with me, talking and laughing, maybe even researching. I didn't care what we did, but I did want to do it with her.

After she left, I plodded around the cottage a bit, half-heartedly looking through the equipment Norton and Kate left behind. Meanwhile, my mind floated from images of Anya the woman, to those of Anya the mermaid. Her hair and eyes, her face, and even her arms remained the same in both likenesses. But her legs melded together beneath the bright scales and the faint scar lines under her ribs opened so she could breathe in her water form. Seeing these things, and hearing her admit to them, didn't make them any more sensible. And after realizing that coming to terms with Anya and Orotava would take far longer than I'd thought, I sat down to lunch.

FIFTEEN: ANYA

I PROBABLY SHOULD have handled Luke and his crew differently, but there wasn't much I could do now. He knew most of the secrets of Orotava and the Obthaluse, and I fault myself for that. I recognized his reluctance to believe me, to believe his own eyes. But I felt he needed to know. He drew me in somehow. I don't know what it was about him, but when I saw him swimming days earlier, diving into the ocean off the bow of the *Sea Star*, I gave into my curiosity. My life, uncertain as it was due to the trench and the light and these humans, seemed connected to him at that moment. It seemed connected even more so now.

By the time Luke came ashore, he'd seen me twice already. That alone left me no way to hide my true form. Granted, I made the choice to tell him about the tribe and the island. I didn't have to do that. I could have easily pretended I was the only one and that no one else knew my secret. But even if he believed me, accepted me as the only one with a changing self, it wouldn't last. It took only an hour for him to meet the first member of my family. His false understanding would crumble in minutes as soon as I introduced him to the rest.

If he could help me in any way with my research, our research now as I saw ways to blend his with mine, I needed him to know the truth. The sea shifts could drastically alter or even ruin my tribe. However, even if he could help, the tribe, and my father, weren't going to be as easily won over as I was.

And while I questioned whether I should have told him as soon as I did, the part that worried me most was Gregorio. He seemed flustered when he found me with Luke and his friends. No one would know it, of course. He breezed into the bar, kissed me, and sat down with a pint in hand. But he grabbed it so tightly his knuckles whitened. Not one to show he was shaken he puffed up. If we'd been in the sea, he'd have swum faster, deeper. But land left him without his usual aggressive behaviors. He couldn't rely on the things he would to do to compete with other mer and prove dominance.

Now, without those practices, he edged around the issue, concealing any discomfort behind a too big smile, a too firm handshake, and a too cheerful conversation. But I may have been the only one to notice. Maybe he didn't even know.

Regardless of who knew what, Gregorio had been pleasant and Luke and his friends left the tavern.

As I walked into the Sword and Dagger for lunch after leaving Luke at the cottage, I rolled my eyes noticing Gregorio on the same stool he claimed the night before.

"Anya, it's lovely to see you. I thought you wouldn't grace my day until I came by the lab," Gregorio said as I sat down.

"Hello, Gregorio. Hey, Uncle Rowan."

Rowan nodded toward me from across the bar.

"Have you had a productive day in the lab?" Gregorio asked.

"I haven't made it there quite yet," I said, not wanting to explain where I'd been instead.

Faking surprise, Gregorio continued. "Not to the lab yet? It's already 12:30. It wouldn't be those humans keeping you from your work, would it? The work the Obthaluse tribe needs you to complete."

"I stopped by the guest house to ensure they were all taken care of. I'm off to the lab right after lunch." I felt like I was reporting my plans to my father.

"Well, I need to know more about your research. The ambassador has questions."

"Maybe we should wait until we can both sit down with Uncle Jinsen then. No use going over everything twice," I said trying hard to get out of the conversation. Gregorio bristled at said the suggestion..

I understood his frustration at being pushed aside. His annoyance seemed driven. But he had no claim on me. We weren't together or even dating. His protective nature was misplaced. I wasn't in danger, and I wasn't his to protect.

As I ate, he turned his conversation to Rowan. I heard my father's name mentioned and I pretended not to pay attention. They continued talking and I heard Luke's name. Intrigued, I listened more and pretended less in order to hear what was said. I couldn't bring myself to give much thought to their discussion, though. My mind went back to Luke.

The man fascinated me prior to our actual meeting. But now that I knew something of him, heard him say my name and laughed with him, he felt real. With all of the tension and questions about the tribe and my research, I should have been focused on those things instead. But I wasn't able to get Luke out of my head.

Was it coincidence that he was here now? I knew enough of the sea to know it had its own agenda. If he was meant to be here, if there was a reason for it, I'd know soon. In a quick premonition of sorts, I realized that when the festival was over, everything else would become clear. But it would be days still until our closing ceremony.

"Anya, did you hear me?" Gregorio asked, breaking into my reflections.

I broke from my daydream. "No, I'm sorry. I've been a little distracted," I explained.

"I know you have, and with the wrong things, too."

On a normal day, I would have spoken up against his comment, but I didn't feel like engaging. I had enough to worry about and I needed to keep the allies I had. Maybe he wasn't truly an ally, but he didn't need to be an enemy either. He was on edge too after all. Our entire tribe had something to worry about now. Those who knew about the trench remained concerned with that. Those who knew about the humans had their worries, as well. And those, like me, who know about both and the light energy radiating from the ocean floor, won the anxiety prize.

"I was saying that your father would be back soon and I'm sure he would rather not find your human friends here."

My human friends? When did Luke and his team become my human friends? Of course, I did spend the day with him and knew all of them by name, but I was merely being hospitable. At least that is what my father would hear when he got back. If he needed to hear anything, that is.

"I'm sure my father will handle their presence here. But that may not be an issue as their boat is being repaired."

"You still don't see the issue, do you, Anya? The real issue. Those humans are now interfering with everything."

"What do you mean 'interfering'? The rift disrupted their research and the electric current failed their boat's systems. They didn't aim for Orotava. They didn't even know it was here."

"That's what they told you? That's what Luke — is that his name? Is that really what he told you?"

"He didn't have to tell me. They were researching, towing trackers behind the boat, when the orbs took out their equipment. I saw it happen. We saw it happen, Gregorio."

With that, I walked out, disheartened with his abrupt possessive and correcting nature. My father didn't speak to me like that, and I refused to allow someone else to parent me that way. Absolutely certain Gregorio would be tossed on his ear if Rowan had heard our conversation, I felt justified in leaving.

My time would be better spent in the lab with my equipment and data, and that is where I was headed. He was right about one thing; I didn't understand the real issue.

SIXTEEN: LUKE

ANYA MAY HAVE saved me from the sharks on the reef, but she left me swimming with them in the cottage.

"Okay, man, what's going on with Anya? Spent the whole morning with her, huh?" Brandon prodded.

Amir, not needing any encouragement, joined in. "Details, man. Come on. We're living vicariously here."

"There aren't any details to give. We sat here and talked about the island. That's it, really."

"Do you believe that?" Brandon asked Amir.

"You may, but I don't," he joked, as the three of us cleaned up the kitchen after lunch.

I held to the story about innocent chatter, not letting on to the secrets I learned about the island and its inhabitants. I also kept my thoughts about Anya to myself. I figured they already knew of my attraction to her, but the depth of it could go without debate for now. Forever, if I had a choice.

I'm not sure what I dreaded them finding out more, that Anya was a mermaid or that I couldn't go five seconds without picturing her, usually naked, on a bed. Or in the sand. Or in the water.

Eventually they gave up on the Anya issue and moved to other business. They asked about the boat, but I knew nothing at that point. With time, we found out the boat needed a complete rewiring. We also found that parts would need to be ordered for our GPS and there was a sizable burn in the hull. I wasn't anything that would take on water immediately, but it looked like one of the orbs may have seared it.

Sitting on the back porch and watching the water, we contemplated the flying, floating balls of light.

"They were light, weren't they?" Amir questioned.

I had to agree with that idea. However, I also brought up the electric shock.

"Well, lightning creates a shock, but it isn't actually light. It's electricity. If we stick with the electromagnetic pulse idea, that explains most of it.

"Unless you add the floating part, the ball part, or the merge to create a sonic boom part," Brandon interjected.

"True," I added. "The part that confuses me the most is that it came from the ocean. That type of energy should shock everything around it rather than surge to the surface. It should spread across the water, not up and through it."

In agreement, there was little else to say, and we passed the rest of the afternoon with cold beers and the beach.

I MADE IT to the lab later in the day hoping to check out the facility for myself. Anya was there, ensconced in her own work, and didn't hear me knock. Alone in the lab, her smile made way to a more serious attitude, and she bit her lip in concentration. Pulled back in a knot, the sloppiness of her hair contrasted with the pristine stainless steel of the lab. Surrounded by whirring and humming equipment, she looked focused, competent, and stunning. I watched her work, moving briskly from one apparatus to the next, stopping only to jot notes.

"So this is where they have you locked up today," I called out, not wanting to get too close before announcing myself.

Taken by surprise, she dropped her clipboard, the clatter echoing through the domed building.

"St. Erasmus!" she hollered, invoking the patron saint of sailors and scooping up her notes. "You scared me."

"I'm sorry. I knocked, but the door was open and Rowan said you'd be here. I figured I'd come down to check out the accommodations." I smiled trying to win my way back into her good graces.

"I'm glad you did. You just scared me. I'm normally alone at this time of day. Happy Hour is pretty popular at the tavern, especially during the festival."

"So I saw. Dropped in before I came this way. Full house there. If nothing else, I figured it would mean there were fewer uh, merpeople, here with you."

"We say *mer*," she said through a smile. "This is when I get my best work done. Show you around?"

She brought me through the central lab, pointing out equipment, talking about her research, and eventually taking to me a tight hallway at the back of the lab.

"Where's this go?" I asked as she grabbed my hand and tugged me toward the hall.

"You'll see, and you'll love it. I promise."

The mystery lasted only moments as we climbed a narrow, spiraling staircase and then I was hit with gratification. The door at the top of the stairs led to a rooftop deck that opened to the sky and the island. We stood amid the tops of palms, looking out over the marina at the elevated end of the island. The setting sun cast an amber glow over the island, creating a candlelight effect full of complex shadows and silhouettes. Anya turned to me, still holding my hand, excited by my reaction.

"This is amazing," I sputtered, awed by the view, the sun, and Anya.

"Isn't it? No one really sees the island this way. Only researchers bother to come to the lab, and most of them are too busy to enjoy the deck. I love it though. I'm up here any chance I get. It's as close as I can get to the isolation of the ocean here on the island."

"I can see that. I've seen hundreds of sunsets, but nothing like this."

"There aren't any other sunsets like this," she said, her voice wistful, as she ventured to the railing.

Looking out over the island, we talked about our research.

"My team and I were hoping to find reasons for the shifts in the ocean floor are occurring faster than in the past and more dramatically. We already found changes of up to 100 feet in depth in spots not far from here," I explained.

"I think I may be able to help you," she broke in. "Well, my research actually. And yours may help me, too. Well, more your encounter than your research."

Excited to hear that there may be some way to enhance what we were already doing, I encouraged her to continue. She began to explain, but changed her mind, grabbing my hand again and dragging me back down the stairs and out of the lab.

She led me to a private dock behind a quaint cottage. At the end of the dock sat a 13 foot Boston Whaler with a compact outboard motor. We were both seated in the boat and rounding the end of the island before I truly knew what she was doing.

"You dive, right?" she asked. "Free dive, I mean."

"Uh, yea. I can free dive. I can hold my breath for about 7, sometimes 8 minutes."

"Good, you'll need to." And with that, she stripped off her dress and sandals. Naked, she jumped into the water. Looking back up at me in the boat, she urged, "Are you coming?"

I took off my shirt, emptied my pockets, took off my watch, and kicked my flip flops to the side before I dove into the clear water. The ocean felt cool compared to the humid summer night, and I followed Anya down below the waves.

As we dove, she pointed below to shifting sand that seemed to be running into a crevice. I shouldn't have been able to see it clearly. The moon didn't offer enough light to break through 10 feet of water, but I could see the ocean floor an easy 30 yards away. We continued to move down, and the light source became apparent. Brightness seeped from one end of the crevice, glowing green. She pointed behind me. I turned, watching small specks of light flowing towards the surface of the water. They glided slowly from the trench, gaining speed and size, coming together, as they got closer to breaking the face of the water.

We also reached back towards the air, and it was only then that I noticed her gills working and the scales on her back joining as they moved down her legs.

As I followed the floating light, reaching the air and refilling my lungs, I saw close to the same phenomena I remembered from the *Sea Star*. The smallest specks drifted in the wind, but also seemed to magnetically attract to other orbs. With the orbs growing, Anya urged me to remain in the water and far away from the boat. Just then, the lights collided with the same sharp, metallic sound as before. However, instead of knocking me out, I watched luminous shards splinter across the ocean spray where they floated back to the water, regrouping as they went. But rather than rise into the air again, they sank back into the sea.

"That," I blurted out, pointing at the shrapnel of the explosion, "is what I saw. That's what knocked me out and took down the crew."

"Is it exactly the same?" she asked.

"As far as I remember, it is. I mean I didn't see it from below the water. We didn't notice it until it was floating in the air. It looked like embers from a fire, but pure white. And then bam, they picked up speed and joined each other before they crashed."

"Okay, that helps. At least now we know it is recreating the same thing you saw.

Awed, I asked, "But what is it? How can you explain it?"

Stoically she looked at me and answered. "That, we figure, is the breaking heart of the deep."

SEVENTEEN: ANYA

LUKE'S EXCITEMENT AND confusion left me giddy as we climbed back into the boat. I had tried to show Phoebe and Fiona the light in the trench, but there had been only some small embers flickering about. It was nothing like I had seen alone, and even that had been far less than Luke and his crew had seen or we witnessed together.

He and I talked about the phantasm all the way back to my dock, focusing on the intensity, the noise, the absolute whiteness of the impact. There was no outside aura ringing the burst as you see with a fire or an explosion. No shading, no differences in tone or hue at all.

"This is the largest collision I've seen," I explained. "They don't interfere with anything in the water, and nothing on the island, but they've knocked out electrical systems on boats. And apparently they've knocked out a few people, too."

He smiled back at me appreciating my small jab at him and his crew.

"That was larger than the one I saw, too. Well, from what I remember, at least. How often does it happen?"

"I've recorded 27 instances in the last three months, but they vary in intensity and frequency. Nothing seems patterned at all. They happen when they happen, and I'm trying to figure out why."

"We thought, well one theory at least, was tectonic plate shifts. Amir brought it up, and considering the trench in the ocean floor, that could be true."

I thought for a minute, agreeing, but wondering if I bothered to tell him the rest. Sensing my hesitation, Luke asked, "What is it, Anya? Is there more you aren't telling me?"

"The trench, it isn't very deep. And it wasn't there until about six months ago. It seemed to begin at the reef and reach outward. When I first saw the light, I had been swimming the reef. It climbed from below the coral, up along the reef and out to the sky. Just one small orb, tiny really, moving through the water."

"Amir tried to touch one. It shocked him, but just now it did nothing to us in the water. Why?"

"I don't quite understand that, but I can tell you that it is happening more frequently now. And I think that if we can harness this light, this energy, we can utilize it. The combustion could fuel almost anything."

"You've been thinking about it for a while then. That's an amazing discovery. But where does it come from?"

"We think it comes from reactions within the core. But these are much closer to the surface than others we've heard of or seen."

"You've seen this before?"

"You have to understand we've been swimming these waters for thousands of years. We've seen lots of things. There was a story when I was young about the ocean's heart and how it broke because the love to two mer was not condoned by the sea. It was a folk tale, but it explained sea trenches to the youngest mer and the importance of listening to your tribe and avoiding poor relationship choices."

"Oh, so the Romeo and Juliet of the deep broke the ocean's heart? That makes sense," he said with a small laugh.

"It may not make much sense, but it was hundreds of years ago. Like I said, we've seen things. But not this, and not here. There's record of something similar along oceanic trenches that are far deeper than we were tonight. And never with any frequency to speak of."

"And now?"

"Now it happens almost daily. And the light leaves the water. I can't find any documentation, folk lore or otherwise, that offers an occurrence of that phenomenon. I was thinking, this could be an answer to your research though. You're studying shifting ocean floors, changing depths, and maybe this is related. I mean we've seen a new crack in the ocean's floor and now it emits electromagnetic energy. Seems related, doesn't it?"

He took my arm, forcing me to look him in the eyes. I turned my attention to Luke and waited for him to come to the same realization I had days earlier.

"Anya, you may have discovered a new energy source in the ocean."

"Yes. That's what it looks like at this point."

"You must know what this means. By the looks of it, you found an environmentally neutral, clean, self-renewing, oceanic energy source," Luke said, shaking his head in disbelief.

"It sounds great, but it may literally be tearing my island apart. It may be breaking the ocean."

"Whether that is true or not, Orotava won't stay unmapped for long."

With that, we sat in silence at the end of the dock.

I WONDERED IF I had told Luke too much when he finally turned to me. Neither of us made any motion to disembark and instead sat in the boat, feeling the waves move gently.

Cautiously, he began, "So, what do we do with this now? How do we advance your research?"

"I'm not sure, but I know I need to find out all I can about the energy source before..." I trailed off, not wanting to finish my sentence.

Luke looked at me then, took my hand in his, and spoke purposefully. "We will stay here and help then. That's how this is going to work, Anya. The team will stay and do what we do best, research, test, theorize, and document. That is, if you'll have us? I'm sure walking around with six human scientists must have stirred up things for you on the island."

"Of course I'd have you. There have been comments about you and the team, but what my tribe doesn't understand what's going on in the ocean. They don't realize they need you," I explained. "But you don't have time to do that, Luke, and you can't make that decision. You need to talk to the team."

And if they planned to stay, I had some serious talking to do too. The tribal council could had accepted the idea of humans on the island for a few days, but involving them in our research, our lives, would be a different thing altogether.

"No need," he explained. "They'll feel exactly the same way. And you and I both know that this is at the center of our research too."

"Even if the decision to stay may put all of you in danger?" I asked him pointedly. "Is Kate going to sit here and help us, knowing her family is far away and she's in danger?

"Danger? So you really think the trench will erupt?"

"Possibly," I answered. "I'm more concerned about the tribe though and their reaction. And if you do decide, as a team, to stay, for how long? How much can you devote to us before you're needed back on shore? How long until someone looks for you or expects you? Until Lucy has to start her next semester of school or Norton wants to head back to sea?"

"I can't answer that, but I know that you'll have us for a bit."

His gallantry sent my mind reeling as I considered how much risk he willingly took upon himself. He couldn't know how noble his action were, nor how attractive. Chivalry was considerably sexy on this man. Sexy, but dangerous.

"How long until we have to explain to your team that the island is full of mer? You already know, and the longer you're all here, the more likely it is they'll have to face this truth, too. That will put them in even more danger. It may put my tribe in danger. You know that, don't you?"

"Well, let's hope it doesn't come to that," he said, and finally climbed out of the boat.

"But it could, Luke." I pressed the issue, urgency in my voice. "What happens when you head back to land, to human land, and Brando lets it slip that there are mermaids? How does Kate justify to her husband and her son that she is going to stay here and help us without telling them everything?"

"We can be discreet, you know. We're researchers, and with that is a certain amount of discretion." He seemed insulted, but I continued.

"I know that. But your research, your entire job, is to find things no one has found before. To make important and life-altering discoveries. Are you telling me your instinct wouldn't be to document the mer, the island, your experiences? I don't believe that, even if you didn't mean to. Eventually, it would come out."

"You don't trust me. I guess there isn't really a reason you should, but I'm still insulted."

"I trust you, as much as I can. But I have the future of my island and my tribe to think about."

"We may have more than that to concern ourselves with, Anya, and you know it. This could do more than disrupt your tribe and your island. It could open up part of the ocean. I don't even have words to figure what that could mean."

"You think I don't know that?" I asked, my volume of my voice rising. I was waving my hands as I talked now, emphasizing my frustration. "Do you actually think that I don't worry about that? The entire ocean could open up. My island could be swallowed. The coast of Florida could be flooded by tidal waves, washed away even. The whole state could be broken off of the continent. I think about all of that. And more! I think of things I'm pretty sure you don't even know to be possible!" Sitting back a bit, I started to feel ridiculous.

"Feel better now?" he asked me, not shaken at all by my actions. That was annoying.

"Not really. But maybe you understand a little now."

He looked at me, care obvious in his eyes, a crooked smile on his face. "I understand, and I'm not sure I want to think about anything I haven't already. Mass oceanic destruction is enough for me. But I also know that the more danger, the more potential damage, the more you will need our help."

"Okay, but what happens when we fix everything and your team inadvertently tells someone? Hundreds, maybe thousands of people head to my island? Mer are captured and 'studied' in the way humans like to prod and dissect things? I can't risk that."

"If you don't, there may not be a tribe or an island to worry about."

He was right. I couldn't worry about later when right now was causing enough anxiety.

"So, was that our first fight?" he prodded, laughing a little. "It wasn't awful or anything, but I think it counts."

"I think it was."

"And there are sure to be plenty more," he said, taking my hand and leaning back, relaxed against the side of the boat and staring at the sky.

Looking at him in that moment, the moon and stars lighting the sky around us, I felt comfortable for the first time in months. Even after an argument, I felt happy, relaxed even. I wasn't worried about the ocean's heart breaking any more. I wasn't worried about my heart breaking either.

E I G H T E E N : L U K E

WE WALKED BACK up the dock together toward the cottage. The excitement and anxiety from our conversation wound down as the sound of waves hummed a constant and relaxing note. The breeze drew across the flowers and ocean, mixing the two into a tropical perfume.

Stopping at the top of the pier, Anya turned to me.

"Luke, I appreciate your willingness to help, but this isn't your problem. I'm not sure what we'll do, but I know we'll take care of it."

She looked vulnerable standing there. The heroic mer who rescued me, who now readied to protect her tribe, seemed immediately frail and slight. Maybe it was the new discovery in the ocean, or how she looked in that moment, but I found myself drawn to her. I found her attractive before, but now she appeared a possibility in some tangible way.

With that thought, I reached for her, drawing her mouth close to my own. She leaned in easily, meeting my request with a soft and gentle kiss. She pulled back sharply.

"I can't kiss you. I have been making terrible choices, and I don't want kissing you to be one of them," she confessed.

"Kissing me would be terrible?"

"No, kissing you would be wonderful. But the choice to do it would be terrible. Don't we have enough to worry about without complicating it?"

"Everything's complicated, you know. So what other choices have you been making?"

She blushed and turned away, obviously embarrassed. I didn't press the issue, but I was curious.

"I just haven't been thinking very clearly lately. Not thinking things through," she said.

"Well, situations of high stress will do that," I offered, still wondering what she was talking about. Before I could ask, she led me into the cottage in silence.

Her home was airy and comfortable. It reminded of something in one of my mother's *Coastal Living* magazines with rosebud wall paper and white bead board ceilings. White washed shiplap clad the hall walls and there were collections of shells and blue and green sea glass in small bowls on tables and shelves. It was welcoming and soft, just like its owner.

She continued to lead me through the home and we eventually entered a bedroom with a large bay window facing the water. She sat me on the bed and stepped back. We had both redressed in the boat, and while she was covered in the soft fabric of the dress, I continued to wonder if her scales had all disappeared.

Awkwardly, I asked, "So, this is where the mermaid sleeps, huh?" I had nothing else to say and a head full of possibilities.

She moved closer, and when I opened my mouth to ask her a question, she placed one finger on my mouth, and said, "There are too many questions to answer tonight. I might as well continue not thinking, at least for now."

I pulled back from her, holding her at arm's length.

My head swam. How? How was I standing there with her? How had the woman from the ocean come to land, come to me?

Answering those questions would clear my mind, but that wasn't what I wanted. I wanted her, nothing else.

She broke her silence. Her voice eased over me, filling my head.

"I don't want to think about this anymore," she said.

142

That was enough consent for me, and I bent to kiss her, brushing my lips across hers again and down her neck. Her skin smelled of ocean spray and flowers. I brushed her hair over her shoulder and lingered with my mouth on her skin. Her warm skin fluttered with her pulse, inviting me to touch her.

I continued my exploration, and she tossed her head back with a laugh much lower than I anticipated. Seeing her enjoy my touch drove me. It encouraged my gluttony. I greedily kissed whatever skin I could reach, running my mouth across her arms, neck, and face. I grazed her wrist with my teeth. Kissing each finger, I watched the longing cross her face.

"Anya, is this," I breathed, "what you want?"

She answered by reaching for the hem of my shirt and pulling it up and over my head. She ran her hands across my chest and her lips across my neck, mimicking the movements I had made. Her fingers tripped along my abdomen, lightly tickling and thrilling me at the same time. She smiled up at me. Knowing that she wanted to feel her way across my body enticed me, and I suddenly found nothing more sensuous than making her smile.

As she learned my body, I reached for her, ready to free her body from the the dress she wore. It slipped to the ground, slowly pooling at her feet. I straightened quickly. Taking one step back, scanning her. The necklace she wore hung delicately. Her lush breasts enticed me and her body showed no sign of the scales I had seen an hour before. There was a slight, pale line under her ribs on each side. Her gills, I thought, reassuring myself that she was the mer I knew her to be.

Fascinated by her golden skin and the length of her flawless legs, I pulled her to me. Feeling the vitality of her body against my own, I selfishly held her close. She squirmed a bit, grabbing at my waist and the button on my shorts, her fingers slipping and frustrating her. I laughed at her irritation. She scowled. Getting back to work on the button, she felt my eyes on her.

"Help me," she said warmly. I brushed her hands aside gently in order to unfasten the pants myself.

Seeing me work the button loose, she ran her hands under the waistband and down. I stepped out of my shoes and shorts, leaving them next to her dress and moving with her to the bed.

She moved to the center of the white cotton-covered bed, sinking into the comfort. I took one more opportunity to look at her. Running my eyes over her naked body, the rise of her breasts, the curve of her hips, the softness of her thighs. Her skin glowed with time spent in the sun. The combination of her eyes, open wide and taking in all of me at once, and her laugh intoxicated me as I climbed onto the bed.

I moved to her, wanting to maneuver slowly, to enjoy the last moments of anticipation knowing that I would have her. She reached for me, more eager than I initially thought. Her plan didn't seem to align with mine as she pulled her body to me. The heat of us together made the day's temperatures appear mild.

Anya ran her hands along my bare chest and back, avoiding my stitches and using her newly formed legs to pull me towards her. Throwing one tanned leg over my own and locking her foot behind my calf, she reached to kiss me. My fingers traced her spine, the contours of her hip. And as we kissed, she wrapped herself around me, and I took her breasts in my hands. She arched and nudged me with her hips. I grasped her and pulled her even closer.

My hand ran down across her flat stomach, down to her hip. I moved away just enough to ease into her, tasting her mouth, her neck, her breasts. She sighed deeply and relaxed into me.

Our bodies pressed together as the glow of the moon tossed itself around the room. Moving slowly, I grabbed her and eased her into a rhythm. Pulling against me, attempting to keep me inside, she rode the wave of delight she felt build in her body and escape her mouth.

"Luke, kiss me," she said, and the sound of her voice drove me. I stopped everything and leaned forward, kissing her lovingly until I was at the brink myself.

My motions hastened. She worked to catch her breath, panting in muted whispers, repeating my name while matching my movements measure for measure.

Her voice, her warmth, her body, it was all too much for me. I let out a strangled moan, collapsing onto her with one final motion. She caught me as I fell to her, my body limp with exhaustion.

Our bodies coiled around one another, the fascinating arrangement of limbs reminding me of a sea star.

Eventually I heard the deep, rhythmic breathing of sleep as she clung to me. If I had plans to move from that spot before she woke, they were gone now. I felt the darkness thicken as clouds moved across the moon and heard the ocean breaking onto the beach. I was happy right there, but I wondered how happy my team would be staying on the island.

NINETEEN: ANYA

AS DAY BROKE, sleep slowly cleared from my clouded head. Luke's arm rested across my stomach, anchoring me. Without it, I felt I may float away, adrift on the ecstasy of his touch from the night before.

But my head eventually cleared as day streamed into the bedroom. I hadn't meant to get caught up with Luke. My plan was to save him and get his team on its way. I didn't need this complication, nor did my tribe. What was I going to do now?

There was growing trench in the floor of the sea and a human cozied up in my bed. Neither of those promised a peaceful start to the day.

When I got up the nerve to slither out from under Luke's arm, I moved fluidly and quietly. However, the knock at my front door startled me. I grabbed my robe and ran from my room to the entrance.

"I'm coming," I whisper yelled.

"Come on, Anya. We're waiting," sang Fiona.

"For what?" I grumbled, tying the robe.

Phoebe was the first into the house.

"We've waited, and now we want to hear about the human!" she exclaimed.

Fiona may have let Phoebe in first, but she quickly slipped past the two of us and went directly to my bedroom.

"We can see the human, Pheebs. Come here!"

"Don't you dare, Fiona. Both of you. Seriously."

My annoyance and utter embarrassment started to show and my friends skulked back to the kitchen where I made coffee for all of us.

Fiona set out to interrogate me first.

"You've been missing since Lover Boy here showed up on the island. What's going on?"

"Look, now isn't the time for this conversation," I pleaded with them. "I've had a breakthrough with my research. Luke isn't even the lead story anymore."

"Must be some important stuff," Phoebe contended. "Stuff you might want to share with your friends."

"I'd love to, but there is a lot going on right now. First, the energy I was telling you about is acting up, growing really. It may be the answer to Luke's research, too."

"And Gregorio? We saw him hanging around you lately."

"Oh, Gregorio. I'm avoiding him as much as possible. There is something going on with him. I don't know what it is, but I don't care for it."

"He's talking all over the island about how Jinsen has assigned him to 'stick to you', whatever that means. And he has no issue telling everyone how wrong it is that you welcomed the humans to Orotava."

"Well, that's mighty nice of him, isn't it?" I added loudly, forgetting one of those unwelcome humans was asleep in the next room.

"He hasn't changed much since we were kids," Fiona added, acid on her tongue. "He was a dolt then, and he's a mean dolt now."

"I don't need anyone watching out for me, or watching me, or whatever it is he's doing. And I'd think that Uncle Jinsen would know that. I wonder if my father has anything to do with it?"

"You may not think you need it, but what do you know about these people, Anya? Why are they here? Is it really research? And of what? We can't have groups of people finding out about Orotava."

While I continued my conversation with Phoebe, Fiona moved closer to my bedroom. "She knows more than you'd think. And she likes how he looks in her bed apparently. Woooo-whoooo, girl!"

At that, Luke groaned, rolling over onto his stomach, congratulating Fiona's snooping with a view of his tight glutes. While they were still under the sheet, it was enough to set Fiona off on a tangent.

"He's gorgeous! Why isn't he naked?" she exclaimed as I made a bee line to shut the bedroom door.

Disappointed that she missed out on the chance to catch a glimpse, Phoebe pouted through the rest of our conversation. But she managed to contribute nonetheless.

"Anya, we're both worried about the humans, but we're equally worried about your research putting you at the center of whatever may come from all of this. Why don't we all go to Miami, Key West maybe? Let's just be somewhere that isn't here for a while." she offered.

Fiona was ready to pack up and head out too. "That's a great idea. Let's go! We haven't been away in ages, and what better time than when everything is about to blow up — literally."

"What is that going to do?" I asked reluctantly.

"Well, it will put us all out of the way, and we know Nishan would like nothing more than that," Phoebe said, agreeing with her sister.

"But it also puts the island, the tribe at a greater risk. If the energy source is a potential problem, and if I know the most about it, I need to be here to protect the tribe."

Phoebe refused to believe that was the only reason, adding, "And Luke, too, right?"

"And what is Nishan going to say about him?" Fiona considered.

I didn't know, but I could guess, and whatever he said, it would be loud.

"We can't talk about this here," I urged. "Let's go to the lab and I'll show you some of the data. Maybe that will convince you."

"Seriously? The lab? How about the beach?" Phoebe offered.

Fiona looked at us both with mock disgust. "You both know there is only one place to talk about danger and men. The bar."

I threw my robe on a chair and fluffed my hair. Still wearing the clothes from the day the before, I followed as Fiona smiled and led the way.

We kept the conversation mundane until we reached the Sword and Tavern. But when we arrived, we found despite the odd hour, not breakfast, not yet lunch, Amir and Lucy were there talking with Rowan.

"Hey, Anya, your friends here are pretty funny," Rowan called as we entered. "They've been arguing over football teams. And the funniest part is neither of them knows what the hell they're talking about."

"Oh, you aren't Derby County fans?" I asked knowing my uncle's odd obsession with the team.

"Is anyone?" Amir said with a laugh. "I mean I'm all for underdogs, but damn."

"They made a comeback," Rowan tossed back the tall man before adding to Lucy, "and don't you go talking anything more about the damn Manchester wankers."

Lucy opened her mouth to protest, but she merely laughed at Rowan's indignant statements instead.

"Well, he has eclectic taste," I offered to the humans. "What can I say? He likes what he likes."

"And what I'd like," Fiona interjected, "is an orange juice, some of those berry pancakes, and a just the tiniest shot of rum." She brightened, turning up at my uncle who had been serving her the same breakfast for close to 50 years.

"And you, lovely Phoebe?" he asked.

Phoebe smiled brightly. "The same, minus the shot of course."

"Of course." Rowan smiled back.

Spinning on his heels, he headed to the kitchen.

"Aren't you eating, Anya?" Lucy asked sweetly. She had the last forkful of pancakes ready to devour.

"Oh, he knows what I want. I'm here almost every day."

Returning with two plates of berry pancakes and my order of chocolate chip waffles with orange marmalade and whipped cream.

Amir faked shock at seeing my breakfast. "What the hell is that? Dessert?"

"Why not start the day with the best part? I can't stand waiting until after dinner. That's hours away," I said.

"I like the way you think, lady," Amir commented. I couldn't have been happier with his comment, and I hoped my uncle and friends noticed the *lady* he added to the end. Obviously he didn't know we weren't human.

Lucy and Amir, finished with their food, hung around to chat with us. They were polite and light hearted, making me laugh and listening to our stories.

"Oh, Anya, I did have a question for you," Lucy said suddenly. Immediately I was set on edge anticipating her question.

"Well, I was wondering how long the dolphin pods have been coming to the bay? Do they breed here?"

I should have known Lucy would be dolphin focused in her interrogation, and I silently thanked her for her innocent fascination.

Calling to Rowan, I repeated Lucy's question knowing the older mer would have a better idea of the bay's history and the dolphins.

"Well, the four pods shift in the bay with only two here at a time. They've been coming here though for more than 20 years. I got to know their family trees pretty well," he said.

"Seriously? That's amazing. Can you come down to the bay later and introduce me, Rowan? I mean if you have time."

"I should have some time later today. Anya, do you think you could come in for an hour and take charge for me?"

Knowing I had plenty to do, I couldn't resist Lucy's pleading stare, and agreed.

With that set and plans made, the humans left and my friends and I were finally able to discuss what they wanted to all along.

"Okay," Fiona started, "they're gone. Rowan is in back and it's just us. What happened?"

I hemmed a bit, but knowing I couldn't get away with not discussing the night, I started. "Well there was another collision. I'm sure you heard it. Luke and I went to see the trench and --"

Phoebe, in an unlikely gesture, cut me off there. "We don't mean the stupid light balls, Anya. We mean with Luke. What happened with Luke?"

"Well they're both related, really. We were talking about our research and I needed him to see the trench. It was nothing like when I brought you two down there."

It was time for Fiona to interrupt now. "You brought him to the trench? That's insane. You don't know what he knows or may have done. What if the humans created the trench?" She sounded angry.

"If humans created it, they haven't come to see it. And if it was humans, it wasn't the humans on our island right now. He was just as surprised by it as I was. And the light. You wouldn't believe the light!

"It was everywhere, and combing to make bigger and bigger orbs. They floated out of the ocean and then suddenly, before we really knew what was happening, they rammed together and bang!"

I knew my description didn't do the phenomenon justice, but there weren't any words for the white light sharply cracking through the sky.

"And that's why I have to leave you both here now and get to the lab. I promise nothing more exciting than sleep happened last night, and I promise to tell you every detail eventually. But for now, I have to go."

With that, I left the sisters staring at the door.

TWENTY: LUKE

I WOKE UP to an empty house. Anya left a cup of coffee in the pot and a note on the bathroom mirror, "Meet me at the lab after 11."

Throwing on my clothes and grabbing the coffee, I ran out the door, considering whether or not I should lock it. There wasn't much to consider, though, as there was no lock on the door. Mystery solved.

As I turned from the door, I ran smack into Anya's friend from the tavern.

"Oh, excuse me. I was just heading out to meet Anya at the lab," I explained with more detail than needed.

"No problem," he said curtly. "She's not home, then?"

"Nope, just a note. I'll tell her you came by. Greg, right?"

"It's Gregorio. A note? To you? If it's all the same to you, I think I'll head to the lab too."

As awkward as it was, I couldn't exactly tell the mer to go away. At least he wasn't asking me why I was at her house.

"And how long do you plan to stay on our lovely island, Luke? Are you and your team heading out soon?"

"We were hoping to get parts for our boat in the next day or so, but beyond that we've no plans yet. Maybe we'll stick around. I'm sure we could help somehow."

"Help? Help with what?" he asked. "I think you'd be best heading out. What could you possibly do that we cannot do ourselves?"

"I don't think there is anything you can't do, pal. But if there is a chance that we can offer support or ideas or manpower, we may stay to do so."

"That won't be needed. You'll want to leave as soon as possible. Today would be ideal," he announced definitively as we reached the lab door. And as he finished that statement, he broke into a large smile and cooed at Anya, "Good morning, darling. I'm happy to see you're so focused today."

Surprised, Anya's eyes went wide, maybe at the sight of him, maybe at me, but most likely at the idea of the two of us together.

"Your friend was so kind as to walk with me this morning. Did you know he entertains the idea of staying on the island — to help us?" He hit the final three words with a bit more emphasis than I cared to hear, but she took it all in stride.

"Good morning to you both. I'm sure Luke has plenty of ideas we haven't discussed, Gregorio. Is there something I can help you with? You don't normally come to the lab."

I watched her smooth his ruffled feathers with well-spoken truths. Not adding to his upset, she managed his emotions and the information he brought with ease, letting him run himself down a bit before ensuring that she would be researching the rest of the day.

"I hope so," he said. "I would hate to think that anything or anyone was distracting you at this pivotal time. And of course, if you need anything, I am more than happy to help in any way."

"I know you are, Gregorio. But at this point, I just need to spend time with the data."

"Will you be heading out as well, Luke? We can walk together," and while his voice was flowery and smooth, his eyes shot daggers at me.

"Actually, I need Luke for a little bit. He is going to run some of his data against my own. But again, thank you for coming by." As she spoke, she moved to the lab door, ushering him out. She had some impressive conflict avoidance strategies. I could learn something from her there for sure.

Once he left, she turned to me. Now alone in the lab, she reached up to kiss me. "Good morning," she said warmly.

"Well, that was a far nicer good morning than good ol' Greg received."

"Competing, are you?"

"I'm not, but he made sure to let me know he is. He would love for me to leave right now."

"And how do you feel about that?" she asked, kissing me again.

"I think I'd rather stick around a while and see how many of these kisses you're willing to hand out."

We continued to distract each other with kisses until it was clear our choices included continuing the playful game and giving up on the day, or stopping where we were and moving forward with what actually needed to be done.

"Okay, okay. Time out," she interrupted breathy and flush. "If we're stopping, you'll need to remove your hand from my breast." A large smile spread across her face.

"And if we are going to research, your hands will also need to move away from my abs and chest," I added.

Coming down from our dreamlike state, she turned to grab her notes. "I do have things I need to share with you," she urged.

"What do you have to share?" I emphasized the double meaning a bit, laughing at my own immaturity.

She laughed too, but she also swatted me with her hand and moved to the other side of the lab. I followed, giving myself enough space to cool down, and allowing her a chance to do the same. I knew if we found ourselves within grasping distance again too soon, the day would be shot and we'd be a heap on the floor. It was a great thought, but now wasn't the time.

"I found something interesting in the data this morning," she called to me. "I think it's a pattern, actually. It's just not your typical pattern."

"What's that mean here?" I asked.

"Well, you know how most patterns move in one, maybe two directions? This one doesn't."

She went on to explain the pattern showed that while the frequency was increasing overall, it actually detoured to show a decrease in three instances before increasing. And while they came more frequently, there wasn't a pattern to the recurrence until the twenty-fifth incident. The intensity did increase each time, but only by a small fraction.

After thoroughly explaining the predictions she made, I saw that the intensity would be noticeable to outside areas within the next few months. The folks sitting in Vero Beach, Florida would see the lights soon, and the people in Tampa would notice it mere days after that. This meant the only way to keep the world at large from knowing about the energy was to figure out how to control it.

Anya explained that the few months we were granted to control the light would be cut drastically if anything dramatic was announced at the ebbing. Taking mer holidays into account wasn't something I had figured into any of this, but as she explained the festival and its purpose, it became obvious that she had to consider it. She worried there wouldn't be time to further research if a warring tribe got wind of the trench and energy. Chances are they would try to control the same force.

As we talked, planning how to handle the next phase of the research project, a fax machine in the corner woke with a ring and hum, eventually spitting out one page. I hadn't heard a fax in ages, but apparently mer communication was not done by sonar or email alone. She blanched as she held the page up for me to read:

"1. Humans are a problem. 2. Trisanthians believe the light is a weapon. Feeling threatened. "

"What the hell does that mean?" I asked in confusion.

"It means my father knows you're here, and he isn't happy. And when Nishan isn't happy, the oceans rage. But worse, it means we're in trouble, Luke."

"Who the hell are the Trisate-, Trisanth-, whoever he said? Who are they? Why would they think you created a weapon?" I shot the questions at her rapidly and with more harshness than I meant.

"I told you about the festival, right. Well, the Trisanthians are the most aggressive tribe of mer, and they hold the least amount of land or power. They used to be quite a force, but they came upon some economic strife and basically fell apart for about a century.

"They are often threatened by things they don't understand or haven't thoroughly considered. But when they are threatened, the entire mer society pays.

"They're working to restore their position in the mer world, and they've been doing really questionable things to do this."

"Questionable? What do you mean?" I asked.

"Oh, things like working with some Middle Eastern oil barons to push the mer of that area out of the waters in order to continue drilling. Your basic bad mer stuff," she said trying to be light-hearted.

"Would it have been as bad if they had pushed the mer out on their own? Without humans?"

"It would still be deplorable. We don't turn on each other that way. We have rules to our behavior, and they have kept us around for centuries. And involving humans, well, that is against most of those rules."

"So involving humans is never supposed to be an option?"

"Never a first option. But this possible war could be the ticket to your acceptance here in Orotava. If they know what we're up against, they'll be more likely to tolerate you and the team."

"Tolerate isn't the same as accept, Anya," I pointed out to her, finally realizing how tumultuous the situation was in her society.

"I know, but they'll need your help. They'll see how dangerous it will be for the Trisanthians to get hold of this energy. No one will want that, mer or human, believe me."

TWENTY-ONE: ANYA

"WHY A WEAPON? That would mean we created it, wouldn't it??" I growled after reading the fax again.

"It's just a fax." Luke tried to soothe me, but he didn't understand the issue.

I wriggled away from him and paced out of frustration. "I suppose we could have weaponized a natural occurrence, but we'd have to know what the hell it was, or did. A weapon?"

I could see the issue become clear in Luke's eyes as he did his best to remain stoic. "Well, it is an idea. Just an idea," he said.

"It's a bad idea. A horrible one. How did we supposedly take this unexplained phenomena and turn it into a weapon. They don't even know how it works, or what it is, or what could happen as we study it. They don't know if it would blow up all of Orotava, or the whole Caribbean, or the Atlantic for that matter."

"You're right, they don't know. Neither do we. But we can take the time to find out. And that's what we need to do right now, make a plan as to how we will find out."

"I'll need to call Corvan and Lucinda. Is there anyone on your team that can run data for us today?" I asked without thinking.

The implications of involving more humans in our research efforts was something I could deal with later. However, I hoped what I explained to Luke about the tribe needing him was right. I hoped that when the tribe knew our situation, they'd also know how much we needed the humans' help.

"Of course," Luke replied in earnest. "I'll go get them now. I'm sure they'll be willing to do whatever we need."

And with that, he was out the door.

I refocused and called the mer I needed to contact. The response overwhelmed me and the lab buzzed with voices within an hour.

I tried to call everyone to order, but I fell short and couldn't speak over those gathered in the echoing room. Instead, I urged Uncle Jinsen to grab their attention with his booming, room-filling voice.

"Welcome to all of you," he began. "It does my heart good to see so many of you willing to help out today and on such short notice. I'm sure Nishan will appreciate all you do here.

"Anya has explained to me that her father is now officially acknowledging an environmental issue found in the ocean floor past our reef, the strange and somewhat unexplained light show we've been enjoying off the reef.

"As you're all aware," he continued, "Anya has a plan at this point that we need to thoroughly explain and which will direct our efforts beginning immediately.

"Please listen closely and direct all questions to her after her explanation. And as always, we remain strong by working together as the Obthalusians of Orotava, the ancient and respected mer tribe of the Atlantic and Caribbean Oceans."

With that the group broke into cheers and clapping. I wondered if we should really applaud our potential demise, but now wasn't the time to wallow in that notion.

As everyone quieted, I addressed the group, informing them of the research that I had completed and how Luke and his team factored into everything. I informed them of my father's wish to use the energy force as a weapon, and how I was wary of that decision. There were few questions as they all listened eagerly. Maybe I had explained things well, or maybe they weren't willing to think too far ahead and consider what already rolled around in my thoughts.

Evening came upon Orotava and Luke and his crew had not yet appeared at the lab. The hum of equipment and voices filled my head, allowing little space for thoughts of my sailor. As helpful as that was, I could feel the frown on my face and the lines creasing my brow as I worked.

Mer continued the tasks I had assigned, and Jinsen manned the fax machine and continued the stilted conversation with my father. Crossing the room, he brought a page to me.

"Nereids talking. Rumor of war."

"What?" I exclaimed loudly enough to cause everyone to stop and turn toward me. "War? Over the light?"

This changed everything. I figured the Trisanthians would want control over it at some point, but I figured they'd wait to see what it did first. I thought we'd have time to figure it out, learn to control it, maybe even extinguish it if that were an option. I didn't think they'd come after us for it. I didn't think it was ours to turn over.

"Anya, keep calm," Jinsen ordered in the authoritative voice of a mer used to being listened to. "This is not an official declaration. And the Trisanthians wouldn't know what to do with the light anyway. They may know of it, but they surely don't know more than you do."

As I opened my mouth to speak, Gregorio sidled up to my uncle and interrupted, "Unless they do know more." His voice dripped with contempt.

"How? How would they know more than we do? We've been researching for months and they've just heard about the light."

"So beautiful, but so naive you are, Anya," he spat.

I wanted to slap the glib look off his face.

He continued. "What if they caused this situation, this light? What if they sent the humans? There is plenty we don't understand, and the role of the humans and the Trisanthians is a large part of what we need to figure out."

"I've told you, the humans don't mean us harm in any way. They were stranded. They didn't look for the island, or us. They don't even know what we are."

"Don't they know?" Gregorio doubted. "I know Luke knows about us. Doesn't he?"

"Well, yes." I tried to explain, but I couldn't be heard over the objections of the other mer who had started listening. They stopped researching and were now an active part of our conversation.

As individuals voiced their discontent with me, my head spun.

"Now we're not safe on our own island," someone yelled.

Another joined, shouting, "How could you, Anya?"

"I know we'd rather not let humans know, but he needed help," I retorted, defending my actions. "I couldn't let him die on the reef. I thought he could help."

"You could have let him die, and you should have, " Gregorio added. "We don't need them and they aren't welcome here."

The crowd clamored in agreement, and I sunk into a chair wondering how we would ever handle all of this without Luke.

T W E N T Y - T W O :   L U K E

ON MY WALK back to the guest house, I practiced what I would say to my team. I went over and over it in my head, but I kept questioning how I could ask them to stay when I knew there was danger. But I also knew they would be excited to hear about the research and that alone may sway their decisions. Maybe some would stay and some would return home. Regardless of their decisions, I wasn't leaving.

I found the group on the back porch chatting about the island.

"I think we should delay those parts. This place is paradise," Brandon said, stretching out in a rocking chair.

Lucy caught my eye. "Hey, Luke," she exclaimed. "Nice of you to come on back."

"Hey, guys. You look comfortable."

"No less comfortable than you," Amir added.

Kate dispensed with the civilities, cutting right to the heart of the matter. "Where were you last night? Wish you'd have let us know."

"Come on, give the man a beer before you interrogate him. But yes, Lucas, where were ya?" Norton chimed in somewhat defending me to the crew.

"I'd love one. And I was with Anya last night. I'm sorry I didn't let you know, but I have some important stuff for us to talk about."

"What's up?" Brandon asked with interest. Always the most gun-ho of the group, he was up for anything that wouldn't tip over a boat.

Kate rolled her eyes and began a mini lecture. "Luke, seriously, what the hell were you thin—"

Normally I'd have let her say her piece. I did leave them with no way to contact me, but seeing as how we knew only a handful of what they thought were people, I obviously was with one of them. The island wasn't large, and if they'd asked after Anya anywhere, they'd have found me. Besides, I didn't want to waste time on last night.

Interrupting her, I started with my information. "I know, Kate, I know. I apologize, and you can feel free to harp on it later, but now we need to talk. I'm not sure where to start, so I'll just jump in.

"Anya's research and ours intertwine. She took me out to the reef last night, well, just beyond it."

"Oh, a night dive. I love those. Sure wouldn't have mind going," Brandon admitted somewhat dejected.

"It wasn't like that, Brando. She needed to show me something. The ocean there, just past their reef, started splitting just a few months ago."

"Splitting?" Lucy asked.

"Basically. Where there was what seemed to be solid ocean floor is now a trench, a shallow one, but a trench."

Amir brushed off my comments. "That's not such a big deal. The ocean trenches all the time. It will probably cover up next storm cycle and fill back in. Tectonic shift, man. That's all."

"You'd think, and I did at first. But then I realized the trench was glowing. The bright light that was floating around us and the *Sea Star* came from there. It came from the freaking trench."

"Okay, now that's weird," Kate admitted, not trying to hide her interest. "That's really really weird."

"I know. And I watched the specks of light, the little pieces of energy float around in the water and grow into larger balls. And I followed them up through the ocean to the surface, and they bounced around, coming together and separating. But when they reached the size of golf balls, maybe a little bigger, they zoomed through the air and BAM! They hit and shattered, raining light across the water. It was just like what we saw on the boat.

"But it didn't knock us out. We were in the water, and didn't affect us at all."

Hours later the team stared at me as I finished answering their questions. I had explained Anya's theories and how we may have an answer to our research question right in front of us. What I hadn't mentioned was the fact that we were surrounded by merfolk.

"Okay, we need to see the trench," Kate concluded matter-of-factly. "Let's go. There must be a boat somewhere."

"I'd love to show it to you, Kate, but there is something else I need to explain."

I was dreading this portion, but if I was asking them to stay, to put themselves in danger, they deserved to know everything I knew.

"More?" Lucy asked. "A trench, energy and light originating from the core of the earth, and you say there's more?"

"Yes, and this is probably the most unbelievable portion of it all. Um, well, the Orotavans are not as they seem," I managed to spit out.

Norton spoke truthfully, swigging back the last of his beer and answering, "Who is, pal? Who is?"

"Well, it is a bit more than you'd think. They, uh, they're... I don't know if you'll even believe me, but they're..." I couldn't bring myself to say anything else.

Amir, annoyed at my hemming and hawing, interrupted me. "Just spit it out. Damn, man."

"I know, it's just that. Well, they're mer."

"Mer?" Brandon questioned. "Mer what?"

"Mermaids. Mermen. Merpeople," I conceded. "Mer. They're mer."

Kate, ever quick to recover, was the first to comment after a minute or two of silence. "Don't be an ass, Luke. Mermaids? How much have you had to drink?"

"Nothing, Kate. Not a drop. They're mer. Anya rescued me in the reef in mermaid form. She made the sharks turn back when I was all but a snack. And she transformed in a cave off the beach. Her tail is beautiful, glorious really. It's like a sapphire, no, an aquamarine, all green-blue and matches her eyes. And she has scales that are a little darker and in the shape of a starfish near what

175

would be her ankle. She has slits under her ribs where her gills open. They look like old scars, all whitish pink, when she's in human form."

I continued on, not bothering to take more than a breath. "She followed the boat for almost a week to see what we were doing near the island. She saw the light take out the boat, and she has tried to help us the entire time. With the boat, with our research. She saved my life. And now she needs us. But I can't ask you to stay. You don't know her like I do, and you don't owe her."

Lucy caught my eye then, her face pleading for me to stop my rant and allow them to catch up. But I couldn't. I couldn't let any of them speak before I explained the last bit of information.

"Her tribe is in trouble. There's a chance that the light could take them out. And while we don't expect that will happen, we know that it will be visible to the coast of Florida within months. That gives them, us, very little time to figure out what's happening before humans head out to investigate.

"But beyond the light and the trench," I finally spat out, "they need help protecting the light. Another tribe thinks they created it to use as a weapon, and I'm guessing they could try to take it. Since we don't know what it is or what it does, their intrusion could only make things worse. She needs help to learn everything she can. She needs help protecting her island and her tribe. She needs me. I love her and she needs me."

The last part surprised even me.

TWENTY-THREE: ANYA

LUKE STOOD IN the open door, flanked by his team. The look on his face proved he heard Gregorio's last comment, but he remained undefeated. The crowd in the lab parted, offering him a path to me. He didn't bother to look around the room. Instead he locked eyes with me and determinedly pushed past Gregorio to get to my side.

He reached me and took my hands.

"What do you need us to do, Anya? How can we help?" he asked.

Looking up into the faces of the team, I asked, "Does that mean you're staying?" And with my gaze settled on Kate, I added, "All of you?"

She took a breath and answered fluidly, "Yes, Anya. We are staying. I can't promise how long I'll be able to stick it out, but we know everything, and we're going to help."

"Did you hear that? They know everything," Gregorio pointed out to the group of mer mumbling.

"Yes, I explained all I know," Luke replied. "It is only fair that my team, my friends, know who they're staying here to help and defend. I'm sure you'd expect the same courtesy, Gregorio, if you were asked to help someone. That and probably much more."

"Fair enough, but let's get to that then. What else do you expect? I'm sure you aren't willing to do any of this without some form of compensation," the mer asked with a bite in his voice.

"In fact, we are," Lucy interjected. "Maybe you merfolk are a bit more externally motivated than humans. Who knows?"

"We care about the sea, man. That's all," Norton added. "And Lucas. And he cares about Anya, so we're here. Don't bother trying to shake us."

Leaning over, Luke kissed my cheek and helped me to my feet.

"If you'll have us, Anya, we're here to help."

I looked to Jinsen, waiting for his opposition. However, he merely nodded slightly, the equivalent of rousing acceptance for my generally restrained uncle.

Then, looking to each of the humans in front of me, seeing their acceptance of and concern for me, I addressed my tribe.

"Everyone, everyone. Please hear what I have to say. The humans, these amazing people here, are willing to stay with us. They are willing to continue their research along with ours, to assist us in understanding what is happening to our ocean, our home, and our lifeline. They're accepting of our differences, as we should be of theirs, and they have offered to stand alongside us as we prepare to protect ourselves against the Trisanthian tribe.

"Let's not turn away valuable allies because they aren't mer. By staying with us, they're sacrificing. They're staying far from their families and their own world. How many of you would do the same for strangers?"

A low rumble started as I finished speaking. Mistakenly, I figured it to be voices starting up again. To my surprise, no one had started to protest, however. Yet the sound grew louder. In unison, everyone turned to the lab's large windows facing the reef. There, in our own bay, light danced on the waves as the sound continuously deepened and intensified.

Luke, first to figure out the danger in the bay, yelled above the roar, "Down! Everyone down!" And then, as the light grew larger and closer together, he found my hand in the crowd just seconds before the metallic crash and explosion shook the lab and sent all of us sprawling.

THANK YOU

I hope you enjoyed *At the Heart of the Deep*.

If so, would you mind leaving a review? Readers love to hear what others think of a work, and word of mouth is an author's best friend!

Please look for Anya and Luke's story to continue in the second Orotavan Mermaid Tale, *For the Soul of the Sea*, coming your way in 2016!

Thank you!

ACKNOWLEDGEMENTS

I owe this book to two people in equal measure, Anthony Romero, my amazing husband and friend, and Melanie Karsak, a soulmate of a different kind. Both inspired me and allowed me the not-so-subtle support that every first-time novelist needs. Thanks to both of you for being equal and agreeable forces in my life.

I would also like to thank my children, Danny, Zac, and Nora, for their awe and appreciation. I promised I would finish it so we could go in the pool, and I did.

Andrea Smith, Jane Barksdale, Sally-Anne Cleveland, Angela Montale, Karyn Ott, Martha Wells-Copeland, Dan and Sheila Wells, Joe and Sandy Esposito, and the entire BIC Writer's Group helped me in too many ways to name. Mostly by hand holding, babysitting, and sarcastically commenting when I needed it most.

Lastly, Alex Hollibaugh, I'm glad you're in my life.

ABOUT THE AUTHOR

Carrie L. Wells has been writing her whole life. A winner of the Young Author's award in third grade, she attempted to avoid writing by becoming a biology major. That didn't work as she had planned and she ended up teaching English in a few places before co-writing two textbooks and moving on to fiction. Originally from New England, she moved to Florida with her family during high school, earned a Bachelor's degree from the University of Central Florida and later a Master's degree in English from Hardin Simmons University. She has worked as a journalist, copy editor, public relations agent, educator, retail clerk, and waitress before they were called servers. She now spends time with her husband, three kids, various animals, and a barrage of students in Florida while teaching English at Eastern Florida State College.

KEEP IN TOUCH WITH THE AUTHOR

Email: carriewellswrites@gmail.com

Blog: www.carrielwells.com

Facebook: www.facebook.com/carriewellswrites

Pinterest: www.pinterest.com/clwellswrites/

Twitter: twitter.com/carrielwells

A Goodreads author

About the Falling in Deep Collection

From mermaids to sirens, Miami to Athens, dark paranormal romance to contemporary stories with steam, the fifteen award-winning and best-selling authors of the Falling in Deep Collection are bringing you mermaid tales.

The Falling in Deep Collection (May – September Releases)
Scales by Pauline Creeden
Ink: A Mermaid Romance by Melanie Karsak
Of Ocean and Ash by A. R. Draeger
Deep Breath by J. M. Miller
At the Heart of the Deep by Carrie Wells
The Mermaid's Den by Ella Malone
The Water is Sweeter by Eli Constant
The Glass Mermaid by Poppy Lawless
An Officer & a Mermaid by Blaire Edens
How to be a Mermaid by Erin Hayes
Cold Water Bridegroom by B. Brumley
A Beyond the Sea Prequel by Emily Goodwin
Immersed by Katie Hayoz
Siren's Kiss by Margo Bond Collins
To Each His Own by Anna Albergucci

Never miss a release! Join our newsletter for behind the scenes information and release updates: Join the Mermaids!
http://eepurl.com/bdRtbD

NOW ENJOY A
SNEAK PEEK FROM:

Ink: A Mermaid
Romance

by Melanie Karsak
Out Now

THE FIRST BOMB EXPLODED WITH a flash of white oxygen bubbles. A sharp, piercing sound followed. I felt like my skull would burst. Even though the pain threatened to deafen me, I suppressed my scream. Biting my lip, I tasted blood, and my shimmering blue tail curled. I squinted hard, covering my ears with my hands. My whole body shook, and I knew it wasn't over yet. Five more bombs dropped into the water. The dolphins near the fishing vessel whistled in agony, and then became silent.

I rocked in the water, the ripple of shockwaves rolling past me. Every muscle in my body tensed. When the pain softened, I opened my eyes to see the bottom of the commercial fishing vessel gliding through the water, the prop on slow. Bobbing on the waves, the dolphins floated immobilized. Below the dolphins, tuna huddled, ripe for the picking.

Of course, they weren't all dolphins. Several of the dolphins were, in fact, merdolphins. I scanned the water for my cousin Indigo. King Creon had ordered me to bring her back at once. Something was happening at the grotto.

There had been a flurry of preparation, but I didn't know why. It wasn't as if the king shared his plans with me. Why would he? I was an annoyance to him, a constant reminder of his deceased brother who'd ruled before—and better than—him, a brother whose death had bought Creon the throne.

"Ink?" Seaton called. "Are you all right?"

I glanced over at him. The gruff old merman stiffened his back, his dark purple tail uncurling. Small clouds of blood trailed from his ears.

I nodded. "You?"

"They are using seal bombs," he said angrily. "Illegally."

"When did humans ever pay attention to their own laws?" I turned to the others, the small band of scouts who'd come with me. It was times like this that I missed Roald who'd left the ocean for his exile year. He would have had something smart to say to cut the mood. But Roald was not there, and the rest of us were far too serious to make jokes. "Everyone else okay?"

"We'll be fine," Achates, a hulking merman with dark hair and a ruby-red tail, assured me. He squeezed his blades and glared angrily at the boat overhead. There was no one we hated more than the fishermen...well, except the oilmen. It was no wonder the mermaids of old hypnotized and drowned humans for fun. Of course, that was before my great-great-grandfather King Tricus outlawed siren song. His daughter, Princess Tigonea, had tried to use siren song against her father in an attempt to usurp power. We mermaids still suffered for her failed regicide.

I scanned the water. The bubbles caused by the blasts faded into halos at the surface. Some of the dolphins and the merdolphins, started to recover. We needed to get to them.

The tuna clustered under the dolphins. Atlantic tuna were easy to find if you knew where to look. If you hunted dolphins, you found tuna. The fishermen began dropping their purse-shaped net. It drifted downward like a dark haze.

"Let's go," I called, gripping my blades.

We swam quickly toward the pod, careful to stay far enough below the surface to remain unseen. By sonar, we'd just look like another pod of dolphins. Humans knew nothing about the deep. As long as we were cautious, they'd never see us.

As we drew closer, I noticed that some of the older dolphins had been killed. They floated like plastic bottles on the surface, their white bellies facing the sun. Others kicked and tried to recover from the deafening blast, swimming away in confusion. The dolphins' blood clouded the water, filling my nostrils. This was nothing short of murder.

"Indigo," I called, careful not to sound too loudly. Hearing me, several of the merdolphins turned and swam our direction. I could see from their awkward movements that many of them were injured. Indigo, whom I finally spotted among the dolphin pod, had shapeshifted into dolphin form. Preoccupied with one of the mother dolphins, she had not heard me.

"Can you get them home?" I asked Achates, referring to the injured mers, several of whom had started to shift back to their natural mermaid or merman form.

"Yes, My Lady," he said as he and two of the other scouts led the wounded mers away.

Overhead, the boat motored in a wide circle: halfway done. Soon they would close the net, and we'd be trapped inside. We needed to work fast.

I motioned to Seaton, and then we shot through the water. "Indigo," I called.

She turned and whistled to me in panic. Once we got close, I could see the problem. The mother dolphin had started to calf and wouldn't be moved.

"Ill-omened," Seaton grumbled. "Nothing can be done here, Lady Indigo. You have to go. They are dropping the net."

Indigo shook her head, and then stared at me, making direct eye contact. Against my better judgment, I knew what had to be done.

"We have to cut the net," I told Seaton.

"Dangerous work," the merman said and grinned. "Best get to it."

"In the meantime, try to convince her," I told Indigo, and then Seaton and I set off. I grabbed the net, feeling the rough, human-made object in my hands. It didn't matter how many times drywalkers—mers who could shift into human form, mers like me—told me that humans were kind. All I saw was the death and filth and destruction they wrought. They were little more than barbarian apes. Land brought death. Just ask my mother. Who knew where her corpse lay rotting in the dirt? But that death had not been caused by humans. The Gulf tribe had killed my mother. She'd been a casualty of our war. I barely remembered her anymore, just the shadowy memories of her red hair, her dainty drywalker tribal mark, and the way she sang with a low cadence. How unlike her I was with my massive swirling drywalker tribal covering my back. While our marks were different, we were the same lot in life. Now it was my turn to walk on terra firma. My exile year had arrived. That night I would begin my drywalk. I shuddered at the thought, and then turned back to my task. It didn't do me any good to think about it now. Moonrise would be here soon enough.

I stabbed my blade into the net and jerked it. The net resisted. I yanked hard and soon the metal began to cut. Below me, the massive tuna huddled together. I could taste their fear in the water. Poor beasts. We fed on them too but not in such a barbarous way. With a little luck, I'd have them out of there as well.

As I jerked my knife, I stared at the boat motoring overhead. Seaton was right. Everything about this fishing practice was illegal. The purse-seine fishing method they were using had been outlawed years ago. Disgusting. At least merpeople honored their laws, even when we didn't like it.

The torn net wagged with the motion of the waves. As I worked, anger welling up in me. If it hadn't meant having their refuse in my waters, I could just sink their boat and drown them all. It was, after all, instinctual for me to want their death. While our law forbad using siren song, which was nothing more than tuning of sound resonance, I still felt the ancestral tug in me. I would have loved to purr a sweet song and pull them down into a murky death. I could almost hear the tune in the back of my head, humming from an ancient source. The song of the siren was nearly lost now, its banishment causing it to fade from common use or knowledge. I closed my eyes. With just a few notes, it would all be done.

"Ink?" Seaton called.

I opened my eyes. *Careful, Ink.* "Good. Almost there." I glanced back at Indigo. She'd moved the mother dolphin deeper into the water, away from the surface, and had shifted back into mermaid form. Her blueish hair, befitting her name, made a halo around her. She was using merdolphin magic to dazzle the creature, talking in low melodious tones that echoed softly through the water.

Seaton stopped just above me.

"Got it," I said, then slid my blade upward. The net broke in half, wagging like seaweed in the waves.

Seaton and I swam to Indigo who was guiding the mother dolphin, holding her gently by the flipper. From above, there was a terrible groan, then a screech as the gears on the winch sprang to life. The net wall moved like it was alive, the tentacles of a great sea monster closing in on us.

"We must hurry," Seaton said.

Moving quickly, we swam through the tear and out of the net, back into the safety of the open ocean.

The gears on the winch lurched. Water pressure pulled the tear, causing the net to rip wide open. The tuna rushed free. I tread for a moment, stopping to watch the sight as Indigo guided the mother dolphin into the dark water below us.

"The pup is coming," Indigo called from the blackness below.

Above, the bottom of the boat rocked, unsteadied by the broken net. The winch slowly reeled the mesh out of the water. It looked like a dead thing, a man-made monster fished out of the living ocean. As the fishermen moved along the rail of the ship, their images were weirdly distorted against the surface of the water. With all my willpower, I sucked in the death-dealing note that wanted to escape from my lips. The massive swirling tribal mark on my back started to feel prickly and warm. Harnessing myself in, I reminded myself that it was forbidden. I turned and swam into the shadowy deep.

NOW ENJOY A
SNEAK PEEK FROM:

THE MERMAID'S
DEN

by Ella Malone
Out Now

"WAIT, WAIT," I CALLED TO my new husband. "You're walking too fast."

"Too fast?" he said. "Really? Can't keep up, Mrs. Flynn?" He grabbed me, cradling me in his arms.

The last glass of champagne at our wedding reception had left me hazy, smiling, and tripping on the cobblestone sidewalk. Tom wasn't in any better shape. He could walk straight, but that last beer tipped him past his usual mellow buzz and pointed him at slap happy.

Laughing at me as I stumbled yet again, he helped me balance, asking, "Why don't you take off the damn heels?"

"No way. There are fish guts on this sidewalk," I said, shocked he'd suggest I remove the gorgeous, white, silk shoes.

"But if you leave them on, you'll be on the sidewalk, too."

He had a point, but I wasn't willing to concede. I struggled to take another step, laughing and lunging at his arm. He caught me in a hug, pulling me close, looking into my eyes. He kissed me softly before he spoke.

"You make my life, Laura Flynn."

Jolted from my memory, I dropped a glass as George Sullivan called to me across the bar, "Hey, Laura, another beer?"

"Dammit," I said, slicing my finger on the glass's jagged edge. "Sorry, George. Have it right there."

Wrapping the small slice with a bandage, I poured the draft and carried it over to George who was looking up at the television in the corner.

"Looks like a real Nor'Easter starting up," he grumbled in his thick Boston accent. "Wind's coming in fast."

After fifteen years in Salisbury, Massachusetts, I could finally understand almost everything the guys said. I'd even adopted a bit of their cropped speech, leaving the *r* off words here and there.

"Sounds like it. Channel 9's been talking about it all day."

And it had. So much so that I was already sick of hearing about the storm and it hadn't even hit. Granted, living in a fishing community, we spent more time than probably anywhere else in the country thinking about, talking about, and complaining about the weather.

George looked down as I handed him the beer, and asked, "So, Tommy still out?"

"Yea. I'm not expecting him until tomorrow, maybe later. You know he'll stay out if the weather's too much," I explained. George, a retired fishing boat captain, had known my husband since his childhood and had captained the first boat Tom had worked. He knew Tom to be a cautious and smart captain. And with a storm raging on the coast, if necessary Tom would stay as far away as possible in order to keep his boat, his crew, and his catch safe.

"Stay out in the brine until the sun shines," George rhymed.

With every rain or snow, I had heard the rhyme cautioning captains to stay at sea during bad weather. Tom chanted the rhyme to me the first time we met. Little did I know it would become a tenant to live by once he captained his own boat.

I smiled at George as he raised his beer in my direction in silent cheers. His face seemed to soften and the wrinkles in his forehead lessened with his first swallow. But even with the alcohol-related rejuvenation, his face grew more leathery each day. He was a walking example of how difficult life was at sea.

Looking out the window, I saw the sky, dark and gray, hanging there, waiting. It suddenly opened, emptying itself violently. The low rolls of thunder echoed, shaking the building.

The bar door opened and a few young fishermen came in from the cold and wet, shaking it off as they crossed to a table.

I approached the men, drying my hands on the towel tucked through my belt loop.

"Hey, Laura," the taller of the two called as I approached. He peeled off his jacket. "Damn rain couldn't wait. I was at the door and bam. Starts pouring. How goes in here?"

"Hey, Paul. I didn't recognize you all sopping wet. You two look like drowned rats." I walked back to the bar and grabbed some dry towels. Tossing them to him, I asked, "What'll it be?"

"I'll take a Coors on tap and a burger, medium," he said, running his hands through his shaggy, wet hair.

"Alright, and you, Mack?"

Lewis McIntyre tore his eyes off the window to answer, "Same here. Really coming down now. Bet a ton of boats are stuck today."

"I'm sure. Nothing we aren't use to, right guys?" I asked with a smile and what I hoped was a relaxed demeanor.

As often as I watched the rain come down and realized Tom and the boat would remain at sea, anxiety seemed to build with each rain drop. I flipped my hair over my shoulder and put on my happy face, vowing to fake it until the weather changed for the better.

The day wore on. I doled out draft after draft, my body weight in burgers, a few cups of chowder here and there, and plenty of chit chat.

The news droned on about the rain, showing large green radar bands moving southwest across the screen.

"This is Scott Nelson, reporting for Boston's Channel 9. It looks like the weather won't be letting up any time soon, folks. Logan has delays at this point, and we'll be looking at that in just a bit. So get your galoshes ready, and consider building that ark. We'll be here all night watching the storms for you, so keep it tuned to Channel 9 for the most accurate up-to-the-minute forecasts."

I put off calling Tom's cell phone until this point, knowing I'd only be able to reach him if he were close to the coast. But, as I watched the last piece of day disappear, I figured I'd check now, just in case.

I picked up the bar's cordless handset and dialed the number I knew by heart. I listened to the four rings before hearing Tom's voice say, "Sorry, can't answer my phone. Laura, leave a message. Everybody else, piss off." He thought he was pretty clever for that outgoing message and despite my protests, he kept it.

"You sound really mean, Tom," I'd reasoned. "Maybe you don't want to tick off your buyers when they call."

"Laura, my buyers are all guys like me. They'll laugh and leave a message or they'll laugh and call back later. Besides, why shouldn't I tell it like it is?" he asked me. "I don't wanna hear from anybody but you."

Other guys were afraid of saying "I love you" or admitting to caring about their wives, but not Tom. He was open and friendly, and he let everyone know he was mine and mine alone.

For our first anniversary he had my name tattooed on his left arm, explaining, "The first year is paper, but the guy was out, so I let him use my arm instead."

He was a wonderful man and an even better husband, and in moments like this, as it was dark and cold, I missed him.

As the rain continued, patrons came in looking for a warm, dry place that wasn't home. After years running The Mermaid's Den, I realized that people only came here when home wasn't as welcoming as the bar. They didn't rush here after work if they had what they wanted at home. But I was happy to have a clean place for folks to meet, grab some good food, and have a drink on nights like this. Sitting home alone was depressing even without the rain. With a storm like this, you needed people around you and good laugh. And as long as everyone was laughing, the night, despite the storm, would go smoothly. It's when laughs turned to hurt feelings and thrown punches that problems started.

The attitude in the bar stayed friendly through the end of my shift. Despite that, by the time nine o'clock rolled around, I was ready to head upstairs to a hot bath and a cup of tea. I still hadn't heard from Tom. I hadn't expected to, but if I was honest with myself, there was nothing I hoped for more. Just knowing he was safe and outside the storm bands would ease my mind. No such luck though, and I was left to assume.

While living above the bar wasn't always a blessing, not running to my car and fussing with the lock in the rain was a bonus. Instead, I said my goodbye to Clyde and Tracey, the two employees closing up that night, and turned to head upstairs.

"Turning in, Laura?" Larry, a regular and captain of the boat *Dead-line*, asked as I finished my shift inventory.

"Yes, sir. The rain makes the day so much longer." I looked past Larry, to the window. I could see, in the light from the street lamp, the fat raindrops as they hit the roof of my car.

"Try being out in it all day. I wish I'd just stayed at sea really. Hell of a fight to get to dock, and we came in early."

"When did you tie up?" I asked.

"About two or so. But it took more than an hour to off load. That's the real bitch. I almost fell into the drink three or four times docks were so slick. My damn greenhorn fell on his ass laughing at me."

"That'll teach him, Lare," I laughed. The thought of Larry taking a dive was too much for me. He was a big man, so the image of a redwood falling came to mind. I could easily hear his men yelling, "Timber" in my head. "Was he hurt?"

"Nah, just his pride. And that cocky little ass could do with being taken down a peg."

"I'm sure. But don't be too rough on him. Don't you remember what you guys were like when you were green?"

"Nothing like these kids, Laura. I swear. They can't find the stern of the damn boat."

I laid my hand on his arm in sympathy. "Tom says the same thing. But you'll learn 'em. They can only get better, right?"

"Jesus, I hope so." His eyes softened as he changed subjects. "Well, don't let me keep you. Get yourself upstairs and don't go worrying about Tom. You know he'll be just fine."

"Your mouth to God's ears, Larry," I said and gave Tom's best friend, and the best man at our wedding, a hug.

My extended family surrounded me every night in The Den, with its rich mahogany bar and framed photographs of the town's fishing crews and boats, past and present. There were a few pictures of our dog, Murdock, one each of the local police and fire crews, and one of the girls' softball team we sponsored. It was a nice bar, and looking at it that night, I decided it was more than nice. It was perfect.

It was where Tom and I had marked so many occasions, marriages, births, graduations, deaths. And while not all of them were easy to recall, the bar punctuated them with warmth and friendliness.

The most recent event at the bar was the funeral reception for Tom's father. Lloyd passed away about a year earlier from lung cancer. The disease riddled his body, metastasizing from his lungs to his bones quickly, and he was taken within six months of his diagnosis.

Devastated, Tom's mother Nancy decided to move to Arizona to be closer to his sister Jeanie, her husband and their four kids, the only grandchildren. When she left, Nancy turned over the bar to her sons. That left Tom and his older brother Eric, who lived in Maine, deciding what to do with The Mermaid's Den.

Their dad inherited the bar from his father in the early '70s and everyone in the family worked there at some point. Jeanie had actually been born in the storeroom behind the bar when the roads closed due to a blizzard. Flynn blood and sweat had built the place, and Eric and Tom agreed that it should continue that way. But running The Den was out of question for Eric and his partner as they owned an architecture firm a little more than an hour away. That left me and Tom. Four or five months before Lloyd had his first biopsy, we bought the *Colleen Marie* from George. We were on track to turn a profit with the boat finally, but I'd been working the bar for our entire married life and knew the ins and outs better than anyone besides Lloyd. It didn't take long for the decision to be made that I would run the bar. Each of them owned one quarter, so they paid me a nice salary and split the rest of the profit equally. It worked out well for everyone and the bar stayed in the Flynn family.

I couldn't imagine a non-Flynn taking over The Mermaid's Den with the door jamb covered in height marks showing how quickly children change into teens and then adults. Tom and his siblings, as well as Lloyd and his four brothers, moved up the wall each birthday. And while not as old or as sentimental, Lloyd notched a small mark in the bar over the ice well each time he witnessed a fight. There was one mark for the fist thrown after the Elk vs. Moose Lodge softball game, and another from the McGuire baby shower when the mother-to-be tossed a drink on her husband's ex-girlfriend after hearing a comment about her swollen ankles. Each piece of the place told a story, and I saw Tom in everything that caught my eye. Maybe that's what made me love the bar.